Mailboxes – Mansions – Memphistopheles

Andrew Barger

For Ky who believed in these stories from the beginning.

Fiction

Coffee with Poe
A Novel of Edgar Allan Poe's Life

Edited and Introduced

The Best Ghost Stories 1800-1849
A Classic Ghost Anthology

The Best Werewolf Short Stories 1800-1849
A Classic Werewolf Anthology

The Best Horror Short Stories 1800-1849
A Classic Horror Anthology

Edgar Allan Poe
Annotated and Illustrated Entire Stories and Poems

Leo Tolstoy's 20 Greatest Short Stories
Annotated

Orion
An Epic English Poem

Website: ANDREWBARGER.COM

Blog: ANDREWBARGER.BLOGSPOT.COM

Bottletree®

BottletreeBooks.com

Mailboxes – Mansions – Memphistopheles

Andrew Barger

First Edition
Manufactured: United States or United Kingdom
ISBN: 978-1-933747-27-9

Printed on recycled paper in both
the United States and United Kingdom
(20% Post Consumer Waste)

Fonts: Arial, Lucida Bright, Georgia

CONTENTS

Introduction 9

Azra'eil & Fudgie 13

Memphistopheles. 37

The Mailbox War. 77

The Serpent and the Sepulcher 99

The Brownie of the Alabaster Mansion 109

Geblüt Mansion 147

Stain 159

Purgamentum fingo est totus EGO animadverto. Litterae est sic plumbeus immerito.

Translated:--

They say everything that can be written has been written. I say we are just getting started.

Introduction

For the most part we—the collective body of the human mind—want to know how the artist does it. From architects to authors, the inquiring mind wants to know where the creative spark comes from and why. We solicit (in vain) the ghost of Leonardo da Vinci to reveal the brushstrokes of his *Mona Lisa* or Michelangelo the source of *David's* unearthly symmetry. We desire to know how the magician levitates the beautiful lady plucked from the audience or escapes from certain death while handcuffed in the watery chamber. E.T.A. Hoffmann, whose excellent horror story "The Deserted House" was selected for *The Best Horror Short Stories 1800-1849*, marveled at Beethoven's *Fifth Symphony* in an 1810 review by calling it "one of the most important works of the age."

Regardless of the time or place, a deep part of us refuses to believe there is a little wizard in the Land of Oz who is ratcheting levers behind the curtain. The creative spark must be something more spectacular, bordering on the supernatural. Edgar Allan Poe, in his "Mesmeric Revelation," equated the mind (or the thinking mind), to God: "The unparticled matter, or God, in quiescence, is (as nearly as we can conceive it) what men call mind. And the power of self-movement (equivalent in effect to human volition) is, in the unparticled matter, the result of its unity and omniprevalence; how I know not, and now clearly see that I shall never know. But the unparticled matter, set in motion by a law, or quality, existing within itself, is thinking."

Composing. Painting. Sculpting.

Literature is no different from these other art forms when it comes to taking a peek behind the mighty curtain of thought. We want to know how an author got an idea for a story or poem. Edgar Allan Poe knew this over a hundred and fifty years ago when he published "The Philosophy of Composition" in the April 1846 edition of *Graham's Magazine*. There he gave welcomed insight as to how he created his fantastic poem "The Raven." Poe did this not for the edification of readers, but to aid in the creation of future literature. And in doing so poets have been forever grateful though most have fallen miserably short of the dark wizard, even when he has flung open the curtains and shown them his machinery.

Yet Poe never showed anyone how the spark of creativity was lit. This was because he didn't know himself. No artist does. It just happens and that is the best explanation any artist can give. *Sigh*.

I, of course, am no different. Like Poe, I felt it important to explain the point beyond the creative spark—the impetus behind the short stories found in my first anthology by including an afterword.

Above all else I have sought originality in the stories and the prose poem. In "The Philosophy of Composition," Poe pointed out: "The fact is, originality (unless in minds of very unusual force) is by no means a matter, as some suppose, of impulse or intuition. In general, to be found, it must be elaborately sought, and although a positive merit of the highest class, demands in its attainment less of invention than negation."

These are my first short stories and some originated more than a decade ago. As for me I do believe there is a wizard behind these stories, pulling the levers of originality and creativity under clank and whir. His name is God.

Andrew Barger
February 18, 2011

Azra'eil & Fudgie

THE SKULLCRUSHER CRAWLED down the Afghan road, if you could call the unmarked strip of blowing desert sand and pebbles beneath the marines a "road." They were on their morning sweep for buried IEDs. Today they would be clearing a new path out from Khan Neshin in the Rig district of Helmand province. A clear path would enable Special Ops to slice its way into a suspected stronghold of Taliban insurgents.

"Whoa!" said Corporal Vance from the passenger's seat of the Skullcrusher. His binoculars were pressed to the three-inch thick, shrapnel-proof glass. "That bombed-out tank is . . . painted. So are the Jeeps."

"Aren't all vehicles *painted*?" questioned the driver, Sergeant Moore.

"I mean not just painted. Designs on them . . . patterns. No wait . . . Freakin' flowers . . . Hold on . . . That destroyed tank has a plastic daisy sticking out of the barrel."

The marines were on a new sweeping route. At one o'clock on the horizon they saw a wasteland of mechanized corpses rotting in the desert. The closest was a destroyed Jeep compliments of an RPG. All four tires were blown out and a swatch of charred sand fanned out from what was left of its undercarriage. Colorful white flowers dotted its sides.

"Craziest graffiti I'ver saw. Flowers? Should we have a look?"

"This road has to be swept first," warned Sgt. Moore. "You know it takes forever. Let's keep moving."

The MPAP (Mine Protected, Ambush Protected) vehicle, they affectionately called Skullcrusher, was not allowed to travel more than the speed of a brisk walk. Five miles an hour was the maximum for spotting buried explosives. The marines in the Skullcrusher were forced to investigate everything that could remotely be an IED.

Sergeant Moore checked his rearview and immediately picked up the communicator mouthpiece stuck to the dashboard. He proceeded to bark orders to the much smaller Humvee following behind. "You're too close. Stay at least twenty yards back, Pence."

"Aye-aye, Sarg."

"I know how jumpy you get on these runs."

"Jumpy?"

"Back, I said."

Corporal Pence switched off the radio communications and eased the gas pedal. "Sarg isn't exactly Mr. Ice. You see him sweatin' yesterday when we dug out that last IED?"

"We all got the yips," said Private Fudgerié next to him. "Most guys out here are happy to spend a few hours scanning mountain ranges for Talis. We dig up *bombs* that'll rip us into a thousand pieces."

"They never found the hand of that Jarhead who got stupid last month and tried to disarm one by himself," said Cpl. Pence.

"Just his ring finger I heard."

"Yeah, 'cause it got propelled into the leg of Johnson. Lodged in his thigh. Stuck there like it was plugging a dam of blubber. Had to be pulled out with *pliers*. The wedding ring stopped the finger from going clean through," informed Cpl. Pence.

Pvt. Fudgerié got wide-eyed.

"A good day out here is not getting a body part blown off. Nobody stays calm under these conditions. Nobody. Not even Sarg no matter how much he lets on. And especially not you, Fudgie."

Pvt. Fudgerié made a cupping motion with his hands. "Kiddin' me? I'm ready to hold my first skull today. Looking forward to it," he lied.

What about the gravy boat, Fudgie? came a familiar voice in his head. As always, he tried to ignore it.

"You're going to be standing there holding a metal skull while the detonator is worked on," Cpl. Pence reminded with a tinge of smirk. "Touching it, feeling it against your skin. It's like holding a baby made of steel that you can't drop."

Or a metal gravy boat. You hated holding Mom's gravy boat, too, in front of the entire family. Didn't you, Fudgie?

"And you'll be thinking the whole time, What if I drop it or one of the wires gets crossed by the Jarhead working on it and *boom*?"

With that Pvt. Fudgerié squirmed in his seat.

"You will never be the same after your first real one. Sort of like having your first girl, only that's *way* into the future for you. Right, Fudgie?"

There came no response.

Cpl. Pence was not finished much to the private's dismay. "The sand pelts you in all the wrong places as you stand there holding it. That's when you realize you'll never get all of the grit out no matter how many times you shower. The ears are the worst. All those curves and crevices. Like I said, you're just standing there . . . just, just holding that cold IED skull the entire time while your ears itch like crazy—"

"And . . . and the entire family is laughing at you while Mom glares something awful."

"What family, Fudgie?"

The family that handed down the gravy boat, Fudgie. That circa 1812 English china gravy boat with the fluted pouring spout! The one Mom said had been in the family since great-great-great-grandfather Fudgerié emigrated from Paris. The circa 1812 English china gravy boat Mom told you to be extremely careful with. That's the one.

Pvt. Fudgerié flashed back to that unforgettable Thanksgiving Day, a decade ago, when his domineering mother, widow and elementary school cook—Gretchen Fudgerié, decided that in their family a new tradition would be started. In her mind Carl would not become a man when shooting his first gun or making his first tackle on the football field. No, in the Fudgerié household, where any and all events revolved around food of some type, Carl would become a man in ceremonial fashion by presenting the steaming gravy boat with Mom's award winning gravy—per the Sandusky, Ohio County Fair judges who rated it 9.5 on both taste ("rustic with notes of Portobello mushroom and reminiscent of Parisian bouillabaisse") and texture ("chiffonlike")—to the entire family: the aunts, uncles, eight cousins. And he would be dressed in his new seersucker suit, bowtie and red suspenders that Mom had bought him just for the splendid occasion.

So you, the dutiful (and bountiful) son, appeared from the swinging kitchen doors with all of them watching around the dinning room table while Mom Gretchen hummed a tune that strangely sounded like "The Bridal Chorus" by Richard Wagner (that she called "Here Comes the Bride"). Cupped in your hands was the steaming, circa 1812, gravy boat colored in pale lemon and white with mint green band around the middle. The pattern, as Mom announced to all, was "peony flowers in bloom" with "a neck that a Canadian goose would be proud of" and "real 14 carat gold trim."

The family broke into a round of clapping as you neared the table in a slow, one-foot-in-front-of-the-other, approach. To this day Fudgie you cannot remember who said, "I am so proud of him," just before his shoe caught the edge of the area rug on which the dinning room table sat. You only know that the gravy boat slid down your belly and hit your knee where it briefly wobbled in the air before landing upside down on Mom's ample lap with the spout broken off. There you stood with award winning gravy oozing down your new seersucker suit. Remember? The unctuous liquid burned your stomach, and slowly puddled on the area rug beneath you. Half the table was laughing and the other half gasping in horror. Then Mom, cursing in horrid obscenities that made it clear her twelve year old boy would never amount to anything in life and had completely missed his chance to ever become a real man, dumped what gravy was left in the boat right on your head.

"Fudgie?" snapped Cpl. Pence. "I asked you a question. What family?"

"Oh nothing."

In the Skullcrusher, with the trailing Humvee now backed off, Sgt. Moore and Cpl. Vance continued to scan the changing sandscape. The road constantly quavered and writhed in front of them. The beige sea was never calm.

Cpl. Vance pressed his finger against the window and blurted, "There! I see something. A glint."

"Where?"

"Snap. There it is again. Definitely metal. See it?"

Cpl. Vance popped open one of the six hatches that were carved into the roof and stuck his head out. Through his binoculars he got a closer look. He immediately sunk back down into the passenger seat and verified that the object was at two o'clock.

"Affirmative," responded Sgt. Moore. He eased the Skullcrusher over toward the shiny object while Cpl. Vance communicated with the Humvee in back. When the military vehicle got within twenty feet, it came to a rolling halt.

As Pvt. Fudgerié and Cpl. Pence approached, the Skullcrusher was prehistoric with its 30 foot arm extending from the front bumper, opposite end having a scoop with teeth, side exhaust pipes for horns, angular hide of steel formed to deflect shrapnel. Surrounding its v-shaped, explosion proof hull were eight beefy tires including one on the side and back. They watched Cpl. Vance eject from the back door, which was the *only* door out of the Skullcrusher. They stopped the Humvee and followed suit.

Cpl. Vance signaled inside the Skullcrusher and Sgt. Moore began flipping switches to make the arm operational. He then reached down and gripped a joystick mounted in the center console.

The three marines standing outside (and well clear of any potential blast zone) watched the double-jointed arm lift from the roof and extend to a near vertical position. It rotated and bent at the first elbow and then the second until the scoop reached the vicinity of the shiny object.

Cpl. Vance scanned the vicinity for insurgents, gave a thumbs-up to the Skullcrusher, and the scoop lowered. As was standard operating procedure, a foot-deep square was traced in the sand by the scoop to ensure any trip wires were uncovered that may have extended to a roadside detonator. The men breathed a sigh of relief when nothing was located.

Next Sgt. Moore maneuvered the arm so the scoop was horizontal over the shiny object and thrust the joystick forward. The scoop dug out a large quantity of sand. The object sat glistening on top of what remained.

"You got the honors today, Fudgie," said Cpl. Vance as he gave him a pat on the back and smiled. "Go have a look see, Rookie."

Pvt. Fudgerié sighed. He was visibly nervous, a thousand terrors racing through his mind. The private took a long breath and paused before shuffling his way over to the scoop. He stood as far away from it as he possibly could and stretched out his arm.

It gave Cpl. Pence a chuckle. "Hate to tell you this, Fudgie, if the bomb goes off, standing a few inches farther away isn't going to help."

The private paid the catcalls no mind. He slowly reached his hand under the shiny object, closed his eyes, and lifted. Dry grit spilled over the sides of his hands and through his meaty fingers.

Feels like gravy powder, Fudgie, the kind you get in those packets.

Dusty sheets wafted into the desert. At once it occurred to his racing mind that the bomb was not heavy at all. It was actually very light; so much so that it weighed hardly anything.

"Fudgie, I can't believe you," came the shout from one of the marines standing behind him. "Open your freakin' eyes."

"It's a candy bar wrapper! Oh jeez. A blasted candy bar wrapper!" ejaculated Cpl. Pence. "Fudgie!"

By this time the private had one eye open. Usually he felt satisfied holding an empty candy bar wrapper, but not today.

Sgt. Moore dumped the scoop of sand onto Pvt. Fudgerié's boots while the others hooted.

It was common for the team to investigate false alarms in their meticulous and slow journey to clear the path from anything that could remotely be an explosive. Just last week they examined a lump of clay, a patch of windblown sticks, and a kid's shoe inset with a plated buckle.

"Let me see that," said Cpl. Pence walking over to him. He snatched the wrapper. "This is from your stash, Fudgie. Nobody eats chocolate covered marshmallow bunnies out here but you and that's because your mommy is the only one to send them in the entire United States Marine Corps."

"It is not mine," he retorted in an unconvincing fashion.

"The Talis certainly don't eat marshmallow bunnies."

"It's not his because it's mine," said a thin, female voice from somewhere near the Humvee. "What's wrong with marshmallow bunnies anyway?"

The three men standing outside their vehicles snapped back to look.

There, standing in the blowing grit, was a thin Afghan girl with piercing green eyes. She wore a Pashtun outfit—yellow trousers, a long *qmis* shirt that reached mid-thigh, and a ḥijāb head covering. She looked to be about seven or eight.

The marines were stunned that a civilian had gone undetected across the barren wasteland, especially one in a brightly-colored outfit. There would be write-ups and reports to fill out by all of them. Yet at that moment paperwork was the last thing on their minds. What struck them as even more mysterious than the appearance of the girl were the items she was holding.

In one hand was a paint can and in the other a dripping brush. The large tires on the passenger side of the Humvee had been painted to resemble flowers. White petals fanned out from the wheel rims.

The marines stood agape.

"I said that the candy bar wrapper is mine. Don't blame him!"

"Engage. Engage," whispered Cpl. Pence.

"Uh, what's your name?" asked Pvt. Fudgerié.

"Name's Azra'eil. Ask me again and I'll never tell. What's yours?"

The three marines introduced themselves. Cpl. Pence asked why she had painted the tires of the Humvee like daisies.

Azra'eil plopped the brush in the paint can and sat the can on the ground. Hands went to her hips. "Daisies? They're lilies, sillies. Don't you guys know flowers?"

The marines looked befuddled. There was a long pause as the wind tousled the bright outfit of Azra'eil against the desert landscape. Thoughts that the girl could be strapped with an explosive were running through their minds.

Finally, Cpl. Vance said, "We want to help you and those in your village. We have lots of bottled water in the truck. We build schools and bridges. We're not here to take the country over or to divide it into little pieces like many people think."

"Guess you're here on vacation then! As for me, I'm just brightening the place up a bit. Your ugly truck looks much better."

The marines imagined how they would get laughed to scorn at base camp when they rolled up with flowers painted on their tires.

"We saw your other artwork back there," informed Sgt. Moore who had climbed out the back of the Skullcrusher.

"It's part of my personal desert beautification project. Your tanks and trucks are all the same color. They are so drab looking. Just one costs more than all the buildings in my entire village. So I figured, hey if so many of you guys want to come here on vacation, I want the place to look nice. Brighten it up a bit."

"You certainly do that," Sgt. Moore said.

"There is some more of my artwork up ahead," Azra'eil confessed. "Look!"

Off in the distance the marines spotted more destroyed vehicles and colorful swipes of paint that could only be her flowery artwork. Pvt. Fudgerié managed to smile and immediately tried to hide it when Cpl. Pence glanced at him.

"So what's a girl gotta do to get a ride around here, huh?"

The four marines told Azra'eil to stay put. They huddled in consultation near the bumper of the Skullcrusher. On the one hand they were never to pick up a civilian as a safety measure. Thoughts that she could be wired with explosives or have a tracking beeper strapped on her marched through their minds. On the other hand they realized the chances of the child getting blown up by running across a desert that had not been swept were high. It happened nearly every day.

It was Sgt. Moore who thought of a compromise. This was a rare occasion for the battle hardened marine. "Why don't you walk right beside one of our vehicles? We don't move fast."

"Tell me about it. A grandma in a tight *qmis* could beat you guys."

"But we'll have to pat you down first. That okay?"

"Whatever floats your boat," Azra'eil said, raising her arms.

Sgt. Moore motioned to Pvt. Vance who strode over and lightly swatted at the girl's puffing, blowing outfit.

Azra'eil chortled and giggled. She pulled off Pvt. Vance's sunglasses and tried them on. She made fun of his "absurd looking" outfit that needed a splash of color. She told him to smile more. She asked him how making war could bring peace. She instructed him not to ask her name again because she would never tell.

Pvt. Vance finally gave a signal that Azra'eil was clean. He felt drained from the encounter.

Following strict Civilian Encounter Procedures (CEP), they searched around both vehicles, as well as the undercarriages using a round mirror secured to an extended metal rod. They searched the interior compartments and last, the roofs.

There was concern the girl was communicating with—or acting as a spotter for—insurgents. Sgt. Moore put the team on high alert as the marines piled into their respective vehicles.

Azra'eil began walking beside the Humvee right between the two wheels; a yellowy flower between two white ones.

"That was strange," said Cpl. Pence as he took his seat next to Pvt. Fudgerié in the Humvee. "Can you see her out there?"

The private put his window down and checked the side view mirror. "Yep."

"Think she's a little terrorist?"

"I *hearddddd* that!" came the call from outside the Humvee. Azra'eil hopped on the step below the passenger door and spoke in the window, which made Pvt. Fudgerié lean away from her. Azra'eil stuck a leg and arm into the air. "*Weee!* Never ridden on one of these before."

"You are not to be riding on the side of the vehicle," Cpl. Pence warned. "Get off now."

She mouthed the words back to him.

This made Pvt. Fudgerié laugh uncontrollably. When he collected himself he was surprised to see that the girl was no longer there.

"Where is she?" Cpl. Pence

Pvt. Fudgerié checked his sideview. "Got me."

They were about to radio the Skullcrusher when they heard, "Boo!"

The girl's head appeared, adorned in the ḥijāb head covering, upside down at Pvt. Fudgerié's window. She was on the roof, piercing green eyes staring into the cab. They had no idea how she had gotten up there so fast and without them seeing her.

"Off!" demanded Cpl. Pence. He had never felt so helpless in the armored vehicle.

"What are you going to do, force me to peel potatoes back at base camp? That's not what we eat around here, solider boy. You know, when in Afghanistan."

"*Down!*"

The girl finally complied by sliding down the windshield and then hopped off the Humvee and continued walking beside it.

"What gives with grouchy pants in there?" she asked Pvt. Fudgerié in a hushed voice.

He shrugged. "Uh, so how long have you lived here?" Pvt. Fudgerié said and immediately felt stupid for asking it.

"About a year. Before that I was on a tour of duty—as you blokes would call it—in Iraq. This country needs my special attention now. I am a big fan of Afghanistan."

Pvt. Fudgerié glanced over at Cpl. Pence and saw a scowl on his face.

"What? She's cute."

"'Cute,' Fudgie? Haven't heard that word since junior high."

Through the open window Pvt. Fudgerié heard Azra'eil say, "Tell him to quit calling you Fudgie. Tell him I'm going to go sand-ghetto on his desert derrière. He still has time. The paint isn't dry yet."

The private didn't understand about dried paint, but the little encouragement from the girl emboldened him. He turned to the driver. "Stop calling me Fudgie. I've told you, it's pronounced Fudg-aye. It's French. You know, like lingerié."

"Like you've ever seen real lingerié, Fudgie," responded Cpl. Pence.

Pvt. Fudgerié bit his lip in distain just as he had done when the rest of the family sat around the dinning table laughing at him in his besmeared seersucker suit that had gravy oozing down the leg.

Along the dashboard were taped photos of his dog, him catching a fish in parts unknown of the Midwest, and his favorite football player back in the States. In the backseat were his laptop computer, a bag of cured beef sticks, and a wrapped cherry pie from a vending machine at the base. This wasn't the first cherry pie he got out of the machine that morning. The first one he dropped onto the tile floor and the sides began leaking crimson jelly. This caused him to flash back to the gravy boat incident under the stress of knowing today was to be his first time to hold a skull.

"From all the food you bring, you'd think we were going for a month," said Cpl. Pence.

"I eat when I get nervous. It keeps me alert. If I get hungry I get distracted."

"When we have food in my village," said Azra'eil, "I eat when I got nervous, too. So don't feel bad."

"And don't smudge the seats with your greasy fingers, Fudgie. How are you going to hold a skull if we find one?"

"I haven't eaten any chips today," Pvt. Fudgerié responded.

"Keep it that way."

Slowly, methodically, the two sweeper vehicles continued moving across the sand. Next to the rear vehicle was a brightly colored girl issuing Pvt. Fudgerié words of advice and wisdom far beyond her years. And when her mouth took an infrequent break, he heard the handle of her paintbrush knocking inside her paint can.

Within a hundred yards Sgt. Moore announced over the communicator that a skull had been spotted. The vehicles rolled to a halt. This time the spotter was sure. This time the ever-changing landscape had effaced a teardrop area of sand and along with it a copse of green-blue wires.

The area was scanned for insurgents. Once cleared, the double-jointed arm extended and swiped out the area in a rather jerky motion. It scooped out the device. Sand washed over the sides to reveal an arachnid-looking explosive with green-blue legs.

Cpl. Pence gave his partner a hearty slap on the back as they exited the Humvee. He ordered Azra'eil to stay near the vehicles.

"It's not like I'm going to be doing cartwheels."

Pvt. Fudgerié's boots were leaden as he trudged across the sand. He felt he was on his death march or walking out of the kitchen with the gravy boat. After what seemed to be weeks on end, he finally made it to the scoop and peered over its metallic teeth.

There sat the skull.

For a brief instant the skull morphed into the appearance of Mom Gretchen with her bushy eyebrows and cornrow teeth. And then it began singing, “Here Comes the Bride.” Pvt. Fudgerié was no longer wearing military fatigues, but a light blue seersucker suit that had gotten way too small on his plump frame.

From behind—over the music—he started hearing Pvt. Vance urging him to pick it up and hold it so Pvt. Vance could dismantle the IED.

From the roof of the Skullcrusher (none of the marines having a clue how she climbed on top of the monstrous vehicle), Azra’eil called out words of encouragement that Pvt. Fudgerié failed to hear.

Trying to blink away alternating images of the grey IED and a gravy boat pattern of “peony flowers in bloom” and Mom Gretchen’s chattering face, Pvt. Fudgerié reached down and cupped the object in both hands. He was careful not to snag his sleeve on the teeth of the scoop.

In what seemed like hours, but actually only took 47.5 seconds per Sgt. Moore’s watch, Pvt. Fudgerié was now holding the IED with both hands.

Pvt. Vance went to work on the explosive with a type of Swiss army knife that had wire strippers, scissors and screwdriver all in one. After a minute he glanced up at Pvt. Fudgerié.

The fear was palpable in his eyes.

“Keep your head on, Marine. Remember your training.”

“How much longer?”

“Longer? I just got started, Fudgie. Now pipe down and let me concentrate.”

Yeah, Fudgie, pipe down, ordered a voice that had the tone and inflection of Mom Gretchen’s just after he failed miserably at his attempt to carry the steaming, circa 1812 English china gravy bowl with fluted gooseneck spout, which, in Mom Gretchen's mind, would have made him a man if he had only been successful. This would be his second attempt because Mom never gave him another one. That had been the true reason he had signed up for the marines and shortly thereafter the most dangerous squad in Afghanistan. He would prove to Mom and to himself that he was a man.

I can do this. I could have done it before.

But you didn't, Fudgie. You screwed up just like you always do.

No I didn't! I tripped over the carpet.

And you are going to screw up now.

I will be someone.

Mom said otherwise.

She'll see.

Pudgie Fudgie!

"Shut up!"

"What?" Pvt. Vance asked, then turned to Cpl. Pence and said, "Fudgie's talking to himself while I'm trying to disarm this skull."

Sgt. Moore looked on nervously from the cab of the Skullcrusher.

Pvt. Fudgerié was sweating profusely as the merciless Afghan sun poured down on his neck and ears. He especially felt it on the undersides of his wrists as he stood there holding the skull. The relentless, arid wind did little to cool him. Sand flies were biting his earlobes. A streak of sweat raced from his forehead to the tip of his nose. It hung there with the private unable to scratch it away.

"Steady, Fudgie," he heard one of them implore. The words undulated and were garbled as if spoken underwater. Pvt. Fudgerié was focused on the heat.

It's hot as a steaming ladle of Mom's award winning gravy, isn't it Fudgie? Look at the V-shaped hull of the Skullcrusher. It's the mother of all gravy boats. Look. The arm is the ladle. You're holding its little baby. *Don't drop it, Fudgie!*

Not now!

And when was the last time you went wee-wee, Fudgie? Huh? One too many chocolate milks this morning?

Stop it. I've got this.

Yeah right, Fudgie. The metal is hot now. You can feel it burning those sausage link fingers, can't you? Those slippery, sweaty fingers just like the gravy boat did.

The explosive was getting extremely heavy and scorching hot against his clammy skin. Pvt. Fudgerié could feel it beginning to slip. The drop at the end of his nose rolled off and splashed onto the grey metal below in a tiny hiss.

Maybe it was the added weight of the sweat drop or maybe Pvt. Fudgerié spread his fingers microscopically apart that caused the skull to slip—rotating in the air as it fell—Pvt. Vance snatching at hot desert air in a late attempt at snagging the skull by its wires—Sgt. Moore screaming from inside the Skullcrusher—Cpl. Pence diving in any direction that led him away from the bomb—Pvt. Fudgerié whelping in horror. No one is sure.

Just as no one is sure how long the marines stood in the desert trying to figure out if they had died, unsure whether they had become parts-and-pieces and whether pervasive shock and numbness was the denizen of death. Yet they heard no explosion. Perhaps they had all gone deaf from the cacophony. But they heard the whirling of dry air. And they felt no pain. And it struck them all at the same moment that they didn't hear the skull thump the ground.

"You looking for this?" came a high-pitched voice.

When Pvt. Fudgerié looked down, he saw the piercing green eyes of Azra'eil peering up at him. There she lay in a diving position, on her stomach in the sand, arms outstretched with the IED between her hands.

Cpl. Pence looked at both vehicles and they were too distant for any person, let alone a child, to have dove from under one of them and caught the falling IED. Besides, there were no small footprints, either.

By this time Sgt. Moore had climbed out the back of the Skullcrusher and was standing off to the side with an M-4 rifle pointed at Azra'eil. "Put the explosive down," he warned.

The girl turned over slowly so that she was facing him. She placed the IED in the yellow lap of her Pashtun outfit. "You may find this surprising, but I am helping you out here. You need it, believe me."

Sgt. Moore pointed with the M-4. "Hand the explosive to Cpl. Pence there."

"I can paint it for you. Perhaps an indigo blue."

Sgt. Moore told her she had three seconds to do as he commanded. He began counting.

Azra'eil shrugged and pushed the IED up to the marine. The girl stood up and brushed sand off her *qmis*. She fixed the ḥijāb that had gone cockeyed.

Sgt. Moore put the M-4 at ease.

For a few moments the marines stood in awe of the young girl as the wind hummed through the tight nooks and crevices of their machinery. They were truly speechless.

Finally, Sgt. Moore asked, "Where were you hiding?"

"Wouldn't you like to know?"

"You didn't set this bomb, did you?"

"Would I set a bomb and then save you from getting blown up by it? Think about it."

Sgt. Moore felt dim-witted. "Why are you helping us?"

"Helping? You silly, silly boys. It just wasn't right. Not here. Not now. The paint is almost dry."

None of them understood the response.

"We'd like to thank you," offered Cpl. Pence. They knew it was important to gain any comity they could with the locals.

Azra'eil raised an eyebrow. "Let me guess, more bottled water. You really know how to treat a girl."

Pvt. Vance turned to Pvt. Fudgerié and said, "You've gotta have a bunch of candy bars stashed somewhere back there." He nodded over his shoulder to the Humvee.

The marines all focused on Pvt. Fudgerié in the hopes of a positive response.

Cpl. Pence noticed it first. "Look! Fudgie's wet himself. Look!" He was pointing at the marine's leg and the dark color spreading down his fatigues. He forgot about the IED and began laughing hysterically as the others joined in.

By the time Sgt. Moore had quieted down the subordinates, Azra'eil was gone. As quickly as she had appeared, she had vanished.

"I've seen stranger out here," Sgt. Moore informed as they searched under the vehicles. "The sand'll play tricks. People can just up and disappear when they are three feet in front of you. We've lost whole convoys in dust storms only to find them again two-hundred yards away."

Where ever she was hiding—if she was actually hiding—they could not find her. After they gave up searching, it took the marines another half hour to get the IED fully disarmed and dismantled.

Pvt. Fudgerié took no part in the process and had a private talk with Sgt. Moore where he explained he could no longer ride with Cpl. Pence and his big mouth. Sgt. Moore, displaying a rare sign of compassion for the marine, agreed. Sgt. Moore coupled it with strict orders that he sit only on the tarp in the back.

As the team of bomb-sweeping vehicles moved on, Pvt. Fudgerié—stiff-legged—quickly asked about a Latin tattoo on the arm of Sgt. Moore. He wanted to talk about any subject but what had just happened.

"*Servo permaneo bovis provestri.* Save the last bullet for yourself," Sgt. Moore informed.

Cpl. Pence, who was now in constant communication as he was riding alone in the trailing Humvee, added over the radio, "You should get one, Fudgie. *Servo permaneo doughis provestri.* Save the last doughnut for yourself."

The marines burst out laughing.

As they drove, Pvt. Vance scanned the horizon for more shiny objects. At eleven o'clock he noticed another graveyard of military vehicles. They too had lilies painted on the tires and various other parts of their machinery.

"Our girl has been busy," he told the others. "Hey wait a second. I just noticed this. The burn marks are *over* the flowers. It's as if Azra'eil painted the vehicles *before* they got torched. Just like the Humvee. Hey, you don't think—"

Sgt. Moore cursed and hit the steering wheel. "Would you look at that? Pence is creeping up on us again. Pence!"

With a quick burst of speed, the Humvee pulled along side the Skullcrusher.

"Pence, listen to me. Don't get stupid."

He stuck out his tongue and raced past the marines in the other vehicle. Fine desert grains pelted the Skullcrusher as Cpl. Pence jockeyed to the forefront. There was no window gesture or radio communication that could slow him down.

He only held the pole position for a few seconds before a jarring sound pierced their ears. They saw blue-green fire spurt from the undercarriage of the Humvee. It launched the vehicle six feet off the ground. The occupants of the Skullcrusher watched in slow motion as the twisted hunk of metal landed on the driver's side, jounced, and ground to a halt.

When the other marines arrived at the wreckage they noticed the lily-painted tires spinning in mid air. It was an air filled with the acrid smell of burnt rubber and oil. A small but malevolent fire was burning near the back axle.

"The fastest way to get Pence out is to tip it over," Sgt. Moore yelled. He feared if they were not quick in their response, even more explosions could occur.

Pvt. Vance joined his superior in pushing on the roof with his hands.

"You too, Fudgie!"

Pvt. Fudgerié began pushing on the roof with his sizeable back. The Humvee jostled in the sand and settled at least twice before they managed to get it rocking. A final effort sent it back on all fours.

With the Humvee righted, Sgt. Moore jerked the driver's door open. It was almost impossible to see if Cpl. Pence was hurt through the gummy, cracked sheet of glass that was designed to withstand bullet impacts and IED bursts.

Once the door creaked open, Sgt. Moore reached inside and undid the seatbelt. Before the commander could get hold of him, Cpl. Pence fell onto the sand in a crumpled heap of death.

Pvt. Fudgerié looked off into the distance. He wondered if the girl had anything to do with this. Through the billowing sand he saw a flapping pane of yellow, then the girl standing there in her colorful outfit, the wind tousling it to and fro. His first thought was to alert the others (anything to make him a bit helpful on this wrecked mission)—

—but then a peculiar thing happened. She raised the paint can and smiled.

He reflected for a moment, a twirl of coal-black smoke billowing behind him, then responded in like kind through a large grin that appeared in the middle of Pvt. Fudgerié's moon face.

A sheet of grit snapped across the desert. Azra'eil was gone. The private heard the derogatory call of: "Fudgie, get over here!"

When Pvt. Fudgerié turned back toward the Skullcrusher he noticed that the fat tires had been painted into lilies, too.

Azra'eil & Fudgie
Afterword

In this story the angel of death, who has taken the form of a precocious eight-year-old girl, tags along with Private Fudgerié and his team of marines as they sweep for roadside bombs in Afghanistan.

Death takes many forms and manifestations.

It comes for many people when they least expect it. Death visits on sunny days and when people are in the best of health. Death comes to the park and playground alike. Around the time of the first Gulf War when I saw the photos of The Highway of Death between Kuwait and Iraq, I got the idea for a story about a girl who beautifies destroyed war machinery by sticking flowers in tank muzzles, painting colorful designs on the sides of the machinery. She is a ray of sunshine during the horrors of war. At the time I wrote a few lines of dialogue between the girl and various soldiers. That's as far as I got with other projects I had undertaken.

These bits and pieces remained in my electronic filing drawer, bouncing from computer to computer over the years. In 2009 I used those few lines of dialogue to build the story for this collection.

Memphistopheles

O YE RURAL DEITIES, WHOSOEVER YE ARE, WHO TAKE UP YOUR MANSION IN THIS UNINHABITED PLACE, GIVE EAR TO THE COMPLAINTS OF AN UNHAPPY LOVER, ...

Don Quixote de la Mancha
Miguel de Cervantes Saaverda

THEO WINTERBOTTOM DREAMED of killing his wife in a fantastic way, an artistic way of brilliance befitting a poet and a man in touch with his inner self. Ms. Mary Quite Contrary. Ms.-CEO-of-a-Fortune-Ten-Company. Her very title was a major impetus for carrying out the plan.

When this particular vision came true the others would also become reality. He would finally get his picture on the back flap of a dust jacket—scratch that—the *entire* back cover of his poetry collection. Not a mug shot, either; a cool black-and-white body shot of him in a trench coast standing on a pier or walking down the railroad tracks somewhere in Memphis, or an action candid of him climbing rocks or snow boarding in some exotic local. The photo would have to hide the sizeable gut he'd been cultivating. He knew that all too well. Theo figured digital photography could take care of that with a few strokes of a digital airbrush.

Apart from the gut he was good looking, and everyone knows poets who are easy on the eyes sell more copies (the beak-nosed T.S. Eliot being, in Theo's mind, the lone exception).

The photography shoots. The dustcover. The travel. One day very soon it would all become a literary reality.

Who cared what Mary said about his work ethic? He *was* a poet (not withstanding he had yet to be published) and poets needed to let their minds wander for hours at a time to distil their grand notions. He was going to own romantic verse once he got his first opportunity to be read. Heck, other poets would ask him to lease space in it. Homer. Milton. Dante. Wordsworth. Longfellow. Coleridge. Keats. Poe. Theo would stand on their shoulders and the world would know his prose was *better*. *Mary* was the only person stopping him.

He envisioned the book tour where he would sign his name artistically in metallic silver ink or perhaps gold, and while he was at it actually have meaningful conversations with fans explaining iambic pentameter with one flailing hand and anapest with the other in only the way a poet can. He would avoid becoming a robotic signer who merely opened the cover, scrawled on the inside, closed it, and clamored for the next book from the next meaningless fan.

Not that Mary would still be alive to see all this, but a part of him wished otherwise so Mary could actually see him at one of the signings just sitting there with stacks of his books, cute young theatre majors fawning all over him. Oh how he would rub her face in it. He thought back how it had been years since Mary came up to him and introduced herself in that Ole Miss coffeehouse after Theo had been booed off stage during open mike night. She talked to him out of pity more than anything else. She "took him on" like one takes a puppy from the pound, and from then forward Theo became *her* pet project. Theo's poetry had greatly improved since then no matter how poorly Mary treated him now.

Or maybe he should keep her alive so she would come to his signings on the Square, hairnet in hand with rheumy eyes begging him to come back to her. At which time he would ask her if she had hung onto all those handwritten poems, the ones that first got him writing; the seedlings of his prose. She would shake her head and he would laugh inside knowing they would now be worth hundreds of thousands of dollars because of his fame. That's when he would make small talk and she would tell him how she missed him and respected his quatrains and stanzas after all—that he was a man of genius. Then the really beautiful part would happen as he pretended to place his John Hancock on the copyright page of his collection of poems with a wink and a nod, but would really write a derogatory statement, ONE WORD FOR YOU: BOTOX. When she saw it on the way home she would break into tears once again. That would be spectacular!

In the entire scheme of things, however, where poetry was written to be read hundreds of years from now, Mary was small potatoes. Mary and her wondrous life in all its board of director, pampered glory, would be meaningless when he did. He salivated over being the focus on one of those shiny cardboard "dumps," his mug plastered on it, standing proudly in storefronts and loaded with glossy dust jackets, people huddled around, flipping them over to see the cool black-and-white photo on the back. New terms like "press counts" and "first rights of refusal" danced in his head like children in *Nutcracker Suite*.

Theo relished never being rejected by agents again. They were going to be the ones contacting him, begging for representation and offering to reduce their normal fee; no more than fifteen percent domestic and twenty percent foreign royalties. He would laugh in their face. Down with the slush piles and canned rejection letters that weren't even signed by the rejector. The stacks were so thick he could wallpaper his wife's large house with them. Three stacks of poems were under his bed and not so much as a bite. Who were they to play God over the Prince of Poetry?

His wife's money would bring massive advertising and advertising would bring fame, which, in turn, would only generate more money. A sweet cycle. So what if Mary only let him have twenty-five bucks a week to spend. "Oh, it's not an allowance *per se*," she always told him. "Think of it as a marital trust fund." He was going to soon get all of her money, every last dime. She would be sorry, really sorry.

He envisioned writing in unknown places while surrounded by friends: a book of historical quotations, an expanded version of the latest Webster's New International Dictionary (not that skimpy one on his word-processor), a word and expression locator, a thick visual dictionary, a beefed-up thesaurus (again, not like that skimpy thing found on his word-processor), a law dictionary, a medical dictionary, French, Italian, and Spanish dictionaries, and of course Strunk and White's *Elements of Style*. The world would know he was a real poet when he used "aperture" instead of "hole," "conduit" in place of "tube," "gooseflesh" versus "goosebumps," "footfalls" instead of "footsteps." When his name was spelled in larger font on the dust cover than the title itself, he'd know he'd made it and reached the point in his career when his name alone moved books off shelves as fast as they could be printed or the ebook could be downloaded, and no one would really care if the collection was good. They would buy it because his name was emblazoned across the front.

He imagined arguing with his editor over the use of serial commas and how he would insist it was his artistically merited, God-given right to put them in his poems, further arguing their use was grammatically correct. Then the editor would remind him how strange poets could be and that culling the serial commas would remove five pages off a hundred and thirty thousand word collection, resulting in cheaper publishing costs, which would translate into a higher likelihood of sales. First time poets needed all the help they could get. Inside Theo chuckled at this because the funds from his wife's estate would buy him as many commas as he wanted. He would take baths in tubs of serial commas. He would dance naked through a forest of serial commas. He would publish a whole page of serial commas just to make the agent mad. His "Ode to Serial Commas" would be original, fresh, and be remembered by university professors for centuries to come.

Who is to doubt the heartfelt passion in the serial comma?

Theo foresaw wearing keyboards thin with all he had to say, launching his voice across the world; the one true voice, unlike Mary's even though it was the one the papers quoted and was splashed across the 10K and newscasters recorded. It was a phony voice, a replicated one fashioned from the Investor Relations Department of her oh-so-wonderful company with the right buzzwords and powerful phrases that meant nothing in the literature.

Mary's voice had to be silenced once and for all, and Theo Winterbottom had the perfect plan.

Mary entered their posh two-story in Germantown, Tennessee through the door leading in from the three-car garage. It was Thursday evening and her neck was unbelievably sore. She blamed it on the shareholders' meeting as she made her way down the long hall paved in enough marble to satisfy the output of a small quarry. The first thing Mary noticed was the laundry room and the pile of dirty clothes sitting atop the washing machine just as she had seen them early that morning when she went to work.

"That useless—" She bit her tongue while traversing the rest of the hall and made her way into the master bedroom where she slipped off her pumps.

There Mary saw books piled on the unmade bed, surrounded by a ring of food crumbs. Her face cringed in disgust. She let her hair down and made her way into the bathroom where she started undoing her jewelry.

It was more of the same.

Damp towels were strewn about the floor and hanging over the tumbled stonework of the shower. A crumpled newspaper sat by the commode. A dust ball flittered about that felt as big as the knot in her neck. She saw herself roll her eyes in the mirror and cheeks turn flush. That's when she placed her tennis bracelet down on the counter and felt something sticky. *That had better not be*, she thought, but it was. Glancing down she viewed a glob of toothpaste inlaid with diamonds.

Mary stormed into the kitchen and looked over the serving bar to find Theo sitting in his boxers on the sofa in the exact same place he was every day when she came home from work, his gut busting out of his t-shirt. “You’re good for nothing, Theo. Do you realize that? You sit around here all day typing little blurbs on your laptop while drinking coffee and eating snacks in your underwear. You’re nothing but a keyboard jockey who sits around in his Jockeys!”

Nice, Mary, real witty. He continued to say nothing while reminding himself, *What an angel you are, Mary, always up in air harping about something*.

“This place is a pigsty! You did absolutely none of the cleaning I told you to do this morning when I left for work, when, I might add, you were still buried under the covers. It’s like taking care of an eight-year-old. And look at this kitchen sink,” she added, grabbing a skillet. “I should beat you over the head with one of these dirty pots you didn’t clean again.”

Theo remained quiet, a time bomb silently ticking.

"You are certifiably good for nothing. If you weren't the finest thing I'd seen my senior year of college, you'd still be quoting poetry in those coffeehouses, claiming Poe was your literary forefather. Got news for you, you'll never write a *Raven* or *Annabel Lee*. You belong in the poetry coughing ward you're such a hack. I've read your commonplace stuff, Theodore Winterbottom, and you're all Joe and no Poe!"

That's what hurt the most—the belittling of his art. Mary could say what she wanted about him being lax and a dreamer, but when she attacked his prose that pierced his soul. There was nothing more personal to Theo. So what if his college buddies called him the Gigolo from Tupelo. Elvis's home can't be all bad. He loved growing up in Mississippi and his looks made him not have to work as hard as the others. Heck, they got him hitched to an up-and-comer who made CEO twelve years out of college and now he was ready to get all of her money.

"You're so pathetic, Theo. Why don't you say something? That's another thing that infuriates me about you, Mr. Pensive Poet, Mr. Brooding Artist. The delicate golden boy. Why don't you fight back? You just sit there with that stupid dopey look on your face!" Mary wasn't used to having men fold like flower petals when she confronted them. No woman was who had climbed her way up the corporate ladder (slippery rung by slippery rung) and had broken through the glass ceiling fire-glazed in testosterone. "I am so glad I kept my maiden name when I married you. *Winterbottom*," she said in incredulous disrespect. "What kind of a name is that?"

Hickey isn't exactly flattering for a woman, either, he reminisced for the thousandth time while unfolding his legs off the sofa. No other famous poet had the same last name (big surprise there) and he was going to use it to its fullest to become famous.

Down with the pennames as soon as Mary was down in the grave.

"I have given you everything, Theo, including the shiny Rolls in the garage. All you've ever given me is the rolls on your waistline. Who gave you the Rolex on your wrist? Uh, that would be me. Who pays for this house, Theo? Me once again. I can't give any more. Understand? Not under these conditions and your bizarre behavior. You're slowly going insane. You always put your Rolex on your nightstand at night just because a character does it in one of your poems."

It was a sonnet *to you, Mary, and I should have titled it "Ode to a Lousy Fatmouth. The face-down watch is comment on how meaningless time is when love is not involved."*

"Earth to Theodore, that's not normal. And then you keep that loaded gun in your nightstand. How barbaric is that? There has never even been a burglary in our neighborhood."

He issued a halfhearted look of defiance that she quickly steam-rolled after clanging the skillet into the dual-basin sink. "What have you ever given me besides a perpetually dirty house? Ulcers? Migraines? Gossip at the office parties? Some useless poems? All my suspicions about you before we married have come true. You'll never get a real job. I'm so glad I had you sign the pre-nuptial agreement the day before we got married. Thank heavens for the advice of Mom. You will get absolutely *no* alimony when we divorce and I'll relish every penny of it until I meet a real man. The will is also null and void when we divorce. Mom made darn sure of it."

Where there's a will, there's a relative, Theo recognized and grinned.

"You think this is funny, huh? All a big joke? Our marriage is not a joke!"

Bet your Gucci handbag it is.

"The only reason I've stayed in it is because it helped my career to be married. That's why." Mary finally quelled her tirade and darted back to the bedroom in a distraught, tear-choked fluster. Her marriage had failed miserably and her years of denying it were over.

For the next ten minutes Theo heard sniffles, things being knocked around, clothes flung, and finally the cranking of a zipper.

Is she leaving for good this time? Better not be, that would screw up everything. A sigh of relief was breathed when the washing machine rumbled to life. *She's not moving out if she's doing clothes.*

A few seconds later she appeared at the edge of the family room, suitcase in one hand, tissue in the other. "I'm going to Boston for a weekend meeting with our largest distributor. I'll be back around eight on Sunday. While I'm gone why don't you find the time to get up off the sofa and learn how the vacuum cleaner works. It's really not that hard. You just push the red button on the handle. Remember to take the clothes out of the washer and stick them in the dryer. It's not that hard, either." Mary pointed an angry finger at Theo and made sure she had his undivided attention among the strands of his long hair. "If this house is no different than it is right now when I get back, I'm filing for divorce. Hire a maid out of your allowance money if you have to."

Thought it wasn't an allowance, *dearest Mary. Said your spare cappuccino change was your "contribution to the arts on a daily basis."*

"I want it clean. I mean it, Theo. I've had it! The divorce will happen. I'm through warning you!"

He nodded and smiled wanly as she spun back toward the garage on her way out, thinking for the nth time how childlike she made him feel every single hour of every single day. *This trip is perfect,* he schemed. *It'll give me the window of opportunity.*

As the door slammed Theo remained seated, head slumped, a few strands of blonde hair stabbing at his eyebrows. For the thousandth time he thought of how he was going to fight back and there would be no question as to the winner.

He was startled out of his murderous reverie by the phone. He didn't look at the little window on the handset that would have revealed who was calling. He was sure it was Mary calling from her cellular, not out of the driveway, still barking orders. "Yeah," he wheezed into the receiver.

"Theodore, this is your mother-in-law."

She always called him Theodore. He despised that and she knew it. "Hello, Luci." He never called her "Mom" like she had asked early on in the marriage until things got really bad. He loved that. Quid pro quo. At least he refrained from calling her "Luci Hickey."

"I told you the proper form for the copyright notice is the word copyright, your first and last name, and the date. The C in a circle is accepted here in the U.S. but not in every country. Do you think Sabah uses the English C in a circle for a copyright notice?" Before Theo could answer she blurted, "I don't think so."

The chords in the back of his neck tightened. He could almost see her dark, beady eyes peering through the phone. "Good catch," he said through gritted teeth.

"And use 'All rights reserved' after the notice. Some countries assume you are giving the public some of your copyrights unless you specifically reserve them. All this under the big assumption you will get this manuscript published in the first place. I must admit I'm a little doubtful."

Theo made an obscene gesture into the phone. *Like mother like daughter*.

"What are you working on now, Theodore?"

"A few things. I'm actually trying to come up with a good pseudonym."

"Oh please, you're a pseudonym*rod*! Now, let me speak to Mary, Theodore."

He explained about the sudden trip and how she had just left, getting his mother-in-law off the phone as soon as possible was always his *modus operandi*. What did she know about a poetry collection? He had planning to do, planning that would keep him up most of the night putting the final touches on perfection.

The flowerpot he had his arms wrapped around was getting heavier by the second. He struggled with it through the revolving bank door under the watchful eye of the three tellers and a guard who began moving toward him. It was apparent that the flowerpot was hiding Theo's gut and shirt of screaming buttons.

Theo pushed the pot up with one thigh and collected himself while thinking, *Maybe I have more money in the flowerpot than I thought*. It was three years worth of savings from his degrading allowance and it had to weigh at least fifty pounds. It would be enough to get what he needed at the pawnshop. *Bet none of the great poets ever had to lug around a flowerpot of coins . . . except maybe Keats.*

Theo approached the college-age woman sitting behind the counter. Her nametag read: BELIALA, FOR ALL YOUR BANKING NEEDS. Theo heaved the pot onto the ledge in front of her. *Thud!* Her eyes lit. The teller had seen bowls before, ceramic banks of all kinds (including the Elvis ones), a baseball cap spilling over with coinage, and even rainbow-colored socks packed to the brim, but never a flowerpot.

The teller motioned for assistance from the other tellers and they carried the pot over to a machine with a gaping mouth and dumped it. All the while the guard kept an eye on Theo.

"Step one," Theo mumbled under the roar of the coin machine. Getting cash meant there would be neither a receipt nor a paper trail. The money had been laundered before it was dirty. Activity on the account would bring the authorities sniffing around after it all went down. He would have enough questions to answer once the plan was complete.

The paper-encased rolls of metal were tallied and the teller slapped down a little over two hundred dollars. It was more than Theo had expected.

Beliala asked if he wanted the pot back and Theo told her to "plant something nice it."

Out in the car he counted the bills again, giggling to himself. The electronic sign outside the bank told him the temperature had reached the nineties as he left the parking lot.

He traveled an hour east of Memphis, flirting with the Mississippi border, then turned north on a gravel road flanked by poplar trees, a cloud of dust collapsing upon itself in the Roll's rearview mirror. He snaked past cotton fields and tobacco patches and trailer parks and children flitting behind the trunks of huge oaks. Finally he came upon it. He parked the Rolls and piled out next to a wooden sign creaking in the breeze. It simply read: OLE SCRATCH'S.

Theo entered under the *clang-cling* of an overhead doorbell and immediately realized the place gave the word "clutter" a wide-open feel. It looked as though he was the first customer this year and it was the heart of summer. He waded through musty clothes and around rusty wagons. The pawnshop was dimly lit even on a bright day such as this due to a solitary front window striped by wrought-iron bars.

Behind a display case of handguns sat a guy who was apparently Ole Scratch, feet up. He wore overalls and a stained T-shirt that may have been white in a former life. A small fan sat twirling behind him that violated every wiring code since the 1940s. It surprised Theo the place even had electricity.

"Got anything in mind? Most people come in here looking for everything and nothing all ata same time."

Theo surveyed the contents beneath Ole Scratch's feet before answering. One caught his eye in particular. "I'd like to purchase that one with the ivory handle," he said, pointing at the yellowed glass of the case, and that compact handgun."

"A .22 caliber *and* a 9mm? Sounds like yer lookin' fer two-fisted trouble."

"Oh, no sir," Theo immediately qualified, waving his hands. "Just getting some protection for my family. A man can never be too sure these days."

"Two guns?"

There were no background checks in these backwaters of Tennessee. Theo didn't have forty-eight hours to wait, but more importantly it would've created a paper trail he was determined to avoid. Mary would be home late tomorrow.

Ole Scratch could've cared less what the revolver and compact handgun were for as he dropped his feet and slid back the panel to fish them out. The 9mm handgun was the first to appear. Theo took it and was surprised at how light it felt in his hand, which for a second had him believing if he squeezed the trigger a flag would pop out with the word BANG! across it.

Next the wrinkly old man pulled out the .22 caliber handgun with a snake carved on the ivory handle. "Call this'un the Garden of Eden. It's an Astra 200 Firecat."

Theo sat the 9mm on the counter and held up the Firecat in the dusty shadows. A look of sheer delight came across his face. He ran a finger across the carved serpent.

"That'll be one sixty." The shop owner took on a look of elation as Theo pulled the wad from his pocket and counted it off without trying to barter. It was half a month's intake for the pawnshop. When the bills changed hands Ole Scratch unknowingly answered the nagging question in Theo's mind. "You know, if a man wants to finds real trouble in these here parts, Beale Street is the place fer it," he said, handing over two cardboard boxes of bullets and telling him by a wink it was "on the house."

"What kind of trouble?" Theo questioned slyly, wiping sweat from his brow. It was stifling in the shop, air thick and lumbering.

"A man can finds most any sins he desires on Beale Street."

"It's almost dinnertime and it's a couple hours drive. Can I make it before closing?"

The old man chuckled, which could've been mistaken for hacking. "You don't gets out much, do ya boy? Beale Street is open 'til five in the morning every weekend."

The statement got Theo thinking. "Any sin?"

"Any sin," Ole Scratch verified. "They close off the streets and let people run wild. Any varmint can be found, even people like you."

Theo wasn't exactly sure what he meant by the statement but thanked him anyway. Ole Scratch gave him quick instructions on how to use both pieces of malevolence. "Pleasure doing business with ya."

A rumble in Theo's gut made him ask one more question. "Where's the nearest barbeque joint?"

Ole Scratch adjusted his overalls and pointed toward the wrought-iron bars guarding the front window and past the dusty Rolls. "Caddywompus. As the crow flies yonder."

Theo nodded and clanged out the door. A few miles down the road he bellied up to a booth with a plastic table cloth at the "Prancing Pig." He ate a slab of ribs, sucking the bones clean while rehearsing his plan. He was sure to suck every drop of spice from his fingers.

When it came to barbeque Theo was an open book. Any type was his favorite as long as it was a pulled pork sandwich heaped with extra slaw between the buns or a slab of ribs (dry rub only, thank you very much). For dessert he got a slice of icebox pie and then he got back on the road after paying in cash.

When he reached Beale Street, in Downtown Memphis, he parked in a back lot and stowed the gun under the seat of the Rolls. Over the course of two hours he ducked in and out of three places listening to bands as if on a blues sampling tour for a major record label. The music had a subtle way of calming his nerves as the sun began to set over the banks of the Mississippi. A few hours later he ate shredded barbeque pork, sweet cornbread, and fried catfish until he could eat no more. At midnight he figured if any sinning was to go on, it would happen right about now.

Exactly what kind of thug am I looking for? he wondered. Theo didn't need a professional, just somebody who could get the job done; a job that would be laid out in the simplest of fashions. Theo had certainly never hired a hitman. He once had his teenage cousin dump toilet cleaner in his roommate's fish bowl at Ole Miss after the guy had heckled him at a poetry reading. But instead of a fish, a person was about to get killed, his own wife nonetheless. It made him swallow hard as he headed onto the brick-paved thoroughfare of Beale Street. *Can I really pull this off?*

Theo angled toward a group of men wearing sleeveless denim jackets and no shirts. He checked both ends of the street to make sure the cops were not watching. It gave him some initial comfort. From across the way it looked as though the group of men had similar tattoos on their right deltoids that offered trouble to anyone who wanted it. Theo rehearsed his canned story as he wove his way among the drunken college students and tourists. He skirted the skinny kids performing back flips down the center of Beale to earn a few easy tourist dollars.

Getting his first clear view of the men he could tell they were from a local motorcycle gang. Sweat dotted his brow as he approached under the surreal red-orange lights. His pulse quickened. *You can do this. This is the first step toward the long and prosperous writing career you've always wanted and you can most certainly do this.* The terms "boldness" and "Theo Winterbottom" were not synonymous. He was twenty feet away when he noticed he had become incorporated into a herd of revelers making their way to the next bar. The bikers certainly didn't notice him coming.

From behind two blonde-in-a-bottle hairdos he saw the bikers duck into an alleyway. It was the last thing he wanted. Theo twisted his neck and saw the same policemen leaning on their squad cars that were blocking traffic. *What good are they doing there? Don't they know somebody on Beale could be trying to hire a hitman and need some protection?*

Theo's belly jounced when he chuckled.

His brief merriment stopped in front of the alleyway as he tried to peer into the inky shadows beyond the glowing neon lights. He felt his shoulders brushed by the revelers and a cold liquid wash down the side of his pants. "Keep moving!" someone yelled. Theo paid the voice no mind and inched closer to the alley, hearing a muffled scream and then heated words echoing out of the corridor and mingling with the dying sounds of the blues emanating from the clubs. He squinted and saw tattooed arms cutting in all directions through strips of moonlight. Theo found himself holding onto the corner of a building, knees shifting. He heard cries for help. There was no mistaking it. For a second he imagined it to be calls from Mary and it gave him some pleasure. He had certainly found the guys he was looking for to exact his plan. Theo waited for them at the mouth of the alley, knowing if he ventured inside he could be their next victim.

From the shadows he heard the *click-clock* of heavy footfalls coming his way. Before Theo could get a word out he found himself lying on the ground, looking up at a flashing barbeque sign of a miniskirt wearing pig in hi-heels. He strained his neck above the curb and saw the bikers running toward the end of the street. At the corner they hopped on their bikes and rumbled away. It left him with a sinking feeling. He wondered where he would find the hitman.

That's when he heard it again . . . the moaning. Theo staggered up, brushed himself off the best he could and approached the dark corridor. "Hello," he called, "Anybody in there?"

"I need help, mister, real bad. Over here."

"Right now I can't see anything," he explained, making his way into the blackness by dragging one hand against the wall for guidance.

"Please hurry, I'm hurt." It was a man's voice.

Theo fumbled around a garbage bin that smelled of old beer and rotten slaw. He vaguely made out what looked to be a thin man sitting up against the wall, holding his side and appearing to have one eye bludgeoned. The man pressed back as if trying to seep into the wall.

"I'm here to help you," Theo assured, getting him to his feet. "Can you walk?"

The man nodded.

Theo took him back to the safety of the street. Under the pulsing neon lights he saw the man was wearing a camouflaged jacket, black T-shirt, ripped jeans. By the texture of his hands Theo guessed him to be his age but he looked much older. Theo was sure the pummeling from the bikers had something to do with it. He got a cup of ice water from one of the street vendors who called its cart THE PORK PARADE. The man placed the cup of ice over his eye.

"What's your name?"

"They call me Yam," he wheezed. "Don't ask why."

"I saw what those guys did to you. Pretty tough crowd." At first the waiflike Yam was reluctant to talk, which made Theo think he was wasting precious time in his search.

"Is your friend okay?" asked a passerby.

"Oh, yeah, just had a little too much to drink. Bumped his head. He'll be fine," said Theo, waving the tourist on.

Yam lifted the cup of ice to his eye again and began to talk freely. Theo didn't know whether it was because of his hospitality or because Yam thought he scared the bikers off. He told Theo it was a drug deal gone bad. Theo's interest piqued. Not only did the bikers take the drugs and fail to hand over any cash, but they smacked him around for the sheer pleasure of it. Theo believed him after seeing firsthand the set of flailing biker octopus arms in the sallow light.

The thought crossed Theo's mind that he should provide a statement to the police, but again that would've established a paper trail, placed him squarely downtown late at night and, worse yet, a direct link to Yam. Theo knew his chance had come but he suddenly remembered he had only a few bucks left after the pawnshop, lunch, dinner, and a few cover charges. There was an ATM staring him in the face, laughing at him. Paper trail o'plenty, but of course, Mary kept the only access card. "How'd you like to get your money back and much, much more?" he asked Yam.

"You sound like an infomercial, but let's hear it." The desperation in his face was apparent.

Thinking fast Theo offered his Rolex as a sort of down payment. Yam questioned whether it was real. Theo showed him how the second hand ran in a smooth circle around the face instead of stopping at each tick. That how he knew it was real. Yam placed it in his pocket without hesitation. Flashing his wife's business card, Theo then explained how Mary was a rich CEO who had her husband on an allowance.

"That's a crying shame," Yam said, setting the cup of ice on the sidewalk. "Criminal."

Theo informed him he would get millions once his wife was in the grave and her stock options were exercised. He told him the difference between restricted shares and incentive stock option as Yam's eyes grew wide. Under the cover of passing shadows and the rumble of Beale Street Theo explained his plan in exacting detail. Yam liked every inch of it and nodded in agreement while Theo wrote down the address to the house. He assured Theo he had been by the subdivision before and knew right where it was.

Finally. Saturday morning. After parking his car a few blocks away and walking to the house, Yam arrived at the backdoor. Theo was determined not to let anyone see him enter or leave. He showed Yam the basement window he was to break in later that evening and the circular area rug he had left under it so Mary wouldn't be awakened by the glass as it hit the floor. Then Theo introduced Yam to the layout of the house and the exact path he would take up the basement stairs, through the first story, and into the master bedroom, where he made it clear on which side of the bed Mary slept. If Yam had any doubts about how rich Theo's wife was, they were quickly squelched by the tour of the massive house (which Yam said was a "certified mansion") that was chock full of antiquities and fine artwork. Theo handed over the snake-carved, ivory-handled Firecat and instructed Yam to make sure Mary was dead before leaving. Theo could tell Yam was taking a certain pleasure in all of this. He was unused to holding such power. The men shook hands at the backdoor an hour later. Theo knew Yam would be returning later that evening, gun in hand, greed in his eyes.

"Hey, Yam," he said, before they parted ways, "that gun is called the Garden of Eden because of the serpent. You ever read poetry like *Paradise Lost*?"

"Roses are red, violets are blue. That kinda stuff?" He paused for a moment, then grinned. "Naw!"

Theo chuckled as Yam left.

Promptly at eight Saturday night Mary pulled into the garage and barely escaped the kind of driving rain that can only be experienced in the Mississippi Delta. She told Theo she was exhausted as she trundled her suitcase down the long hallway, but that was before she checked the house for cleanliness.

It was *filthy*.

The vacuum sat in the middle of the family room untouched. Clothes were still piled on the washing machine. Soda cans were scattered about. A wedge of pizza was lying facedown on the kitchen floor. Dirty pans were piled high on every counter and encrusted with greasy food. Was that a kielbasa in the corner?

Theo had planned the entire mess. He wanted to actually hear Mary say those words, "I'm divorcing you," and he got his wish a hundred times over coupled with many expletives, a few of which he had never heard before, along with claims that he belonged in a ghetto. He smiled through every terse syllable.

Lightning fluttered in the arched windowpanes and in Theo's mind the ensuing thunder clapped its approval of his perfect plan.

Mary became so tired from issuing her verbal tirade while Theo sat smirking on the couch, she tore into the bedroom and fast asleep at ten, suitcase unpacked, fury in her stomach, still in her dress clothes.

When Theo realized Mary was asleep he did a little dance in the family room and then swigged down a caffeinated soda to keep him wide-awake for what was to transpire. Then he watched TV for a few hours as he did most nights. It was midnight before he went into the master bedroom and snatched his 9mm handgun from the nightstand. He ticked the chamber open to ensure it was fully loaded. He placed the handgun quietly back on the marble surface, stripped down to his boxers and T-shirt, and slid under the covers.

For an hour he lay there next to Mary, listening to the steady beat of rain and blissfully realizing when this was over he could break up the pieces of the story and incorporate them into poems. Theo had always wondered if Mary loved belittling him because she was the only woman officer and the all male Board of Directors, in turn, loved belittling her. Theo realized he would never have a chance to ask her that question and his years of pain would soon be over.

Midnight. In the basement he heard the first sound of glass breaking, but not the second as it was attenuated by the area rug. Theo glanced over nervously at Mary. She remained sleeping. That's when he reached for the pistol and tucked it into his side. He could hear Yam's footfalls coming toward the bedroom. A slim figure appeared in the doorway brandishing a gun that reflected surreally in the faint nightlight glow. For a second Theo wasn't positive it was Yam, but then Theo made out his puffy eye. Theo whispered to Mary, "'Til death do us part," then flashed Yam the okay sign as he stepped into the room. There was no way Theo was going to let him forget what side of the bed he was on.

Before Theo could blink, fire spurted out the end of Yam's ivory-handled Firecat. The noise was deafening and it echoed deep into the posh subdivision, a foreign din of wickedness and depravity. Again and again it rang, a licking curl of gray wafted toward the ceiling. Theo felt the bed pulse with each retraction of the trigger and the flecking of blood on the side of his face.

And then a fourth *pop* sang into the air, not from the doorway but from the bed, from the 9mm handgun. Theo felt the warm backsplash of gunpowder on his hand. Yam never realized what happened as he stumbled ahead and folded into a clump on the bedroom carpet. Smiling, Theo immediately called 911.

He splashed water on his face before the cops arrived to make it look like sweat, ruffled his mane. Theo explained in a distraught manner how a man had broken into their house and tried to kill him and his dear wife. He claimed he was fortunate enough to reach the handgun he kept next to the bed for protection and to shoot the guy in self-defense. He claimed it was obviously a robber trying to rid their house of its many riches. The story had been rehearsed so many times in his head he almost believed it to be true, and no matter how many times the police questioned him as he stood there in his boxers with his moon-shaped gut hanging over them, face bespeckled in crimson liquid, it never wavered. They believed it as gospel and offered their sincere condolences on their way out.

The following day passed in a flash. Between breaks in answering questions from the police Theo meticulously took care of the funeral arrangements, claiming to everyone it was impossible to go on. He visited shrinks by the droves, this time to establish a paper trail. For the next two weeks he cried on the shoulders of distant relatives and received countless sympathy cards, wreaths, and baskets of flowers from people he had never heard of at Mary's company, all the while carrying Mary's will around as if it was an appendage. It was not to leave his person. He even recorded it at the County Clerks Office just to ensure he could prove its existence and establish yet another paper trail. He shaved for once and got the hair out of his face. He granted media interviews where he dropped subtle hints about the poetry collection he was penning in honor of his lovely wife.

Instant publicity.

For the next two weeks he did what he simply couldn't do while Mary was around. He gathered papers on every life insurance policy, restricted stock certificate, incentive stock option, executive retirement pension, savings account, and mutual funds he could find. By his count he was sitting on over 10 million dollars. Much more than expected. His writing career was going to skyrocket when he placed full-page adds in every national magazine. This alone would attract a publisher. He dreamed this as he sat on his couch in front of the TV gloating about how he had literally gotten away with murder when the phone suddenly rang. It was Luci. Bad enough she was his *mother-in-law*, let alone a lawyer. He gave off a big sigh and indulged her.

"Theo, Theo, Theo, I was just reading the police report on the robber who killed my daughter. The name's Yam Perkins. Did you know that?"

"Well of course not, how could I have known that?" he lied through clenched teeth, turning over a picture of Mary and placing it face down on the coffee table.

"Funny thing this robber, he's unemployed. Dirt poor."

"I don't care how poor he was, he deserved what he got for trying to kill us."

It was as if she failed to hear a word he was saying. "What's really strange is the guy wore a Rolex." Theo's heart sunk. He tried to say words of surprise but there was no air in his lungs. A puff of wind died before it hit the mouthpiece. "You know what else is strange, Theodore? It is identical to *your* Rolex."

He thought fast, mind racing. He could see those black eyes of hers glaring through the receiver as he tried to think. "Well, he must've stole it in the house. That's what he did . . . the robber broke into the house . . . came into the master bedroom . . . took the watch from my nightstand where I keep it . . . put it on . . . then tried to kill us before leaving."

She laughed in a sinister way. "That's funny, Theodore, because his shoes were muddy. It was rainy that night, remember? The tracks stop at the doorway of the bedroom and go no further. That's where you shot him."

Theo's hands were trembling.

Before he could hang up Luci said, "Being an attorney I am also compelled to inform you that a spouse who kills the other spouse does not take under the will. He is treated under state law as having predeceased the decedent. Goodbye, Theodore."

The federal penitentiary was located on the outskirts of Memphis. Its cinderblock walls and surrounding grounds were tucked in a bend of the Mississippi River. Lying on his pitiful excuse for a mattress, head propped on his palm, Theo recalled the trial that had garnered national attention and quick justice. It landed him in prison so fast his writer's-blocked head spun. The jury deliberated a whole two hours and that included their lunch break.

He wished Mary could yell at him one more time (or a hundred) instead of the gargantuan prison guards. He dreamed there was no Son of Sam Law so he could incorporate his story into a tragic poem and sell it on the outside. He imagined living in any type of house except a prison house and of having his cappuccino change allowance back. Deep down Theo realized he loved Mary (he had written her a sonnet after all) and what a terrible crime he had committed. There was no poetic glory in his depraved act. He really was the loser Mary had claimed over the past few years. Deep down he knew. Deep, deep down.

And that's when Theo heard the sloppy noise. Squishy and heavy, he scanned the hallway through his cell bars. Approaching footfalls on the concrete. The dim ceiling lights soon revealed a janitor with a damp mop fanning the floor before him. Theo now recognized the sound.

The janitor's shoes were clogged in fresh mud, leaving footprints behind in the most careless fashion, which made no sense whatsoever for a janitor. Theo shot from his mattress and grabbed hold of the bars. His belly hit the metal at almost the same time. He thought he saw a smile as the janitor swept by. A wave of familiarity washed over Theo.

"Hey, hey. You. Wait a minute," Theo blurted.

The janitor stopped and turned to face him. The floorsweep had on the same overalls and stained shirt Ole Scratch wore that day in the pawnshop. A baseball cap was turned backwards on his head with a serpent emblem that was identical to the one on the ivory handle of Yam's gun. Ole Scratch called it a Firecat and the Garden of Eden, right? And those eyes were the unmistakable coal-black beads of Luci Hickey, his mother-in-law and never-ending dagger in his side. The muddy shoes. To top it off, he was the only janitor Theo had ever seen wearing a Rolex.

How could this guy be five people in one? Theo pointed through the bars. "You . . . or all of you . . . or something!"

The janitor chuckled. "I'm all of them and none of them. Luci as in *Luci*-fer. Belial with an A thrown on the end. Ole Scratch. Yam. Ho-hum and a bottle of fire rum. All given names, mind you. Don't care much for any of them."

Theo recognized these various monikers for the devil from the literature he had read. "Why are you here?"

"For all your banking needs," he quipped in the voice of the bank teller, Beliala.

"What?"

To the shock of Theo, the janitor took the mop handle in both hands and did what could best be described in the dancehalls of Memphis as a *pas de zephyr, y'all.* While he spun his voice changed tone and inflection to that of Theo's mother-in-law: "Do you think Sabah uses the English C in a circle for a copyright notice?"

To Theo this question might as well have come from another space and time. When he looked on the floor the © symbol was formed in round streaks of mud.

"Now you're a janitor? You don't fool me."

"What do you do for a living?"

"I'm a poet. You already know that."

"You're a pseudonym*rod*!" the janitor crowed in the voice of Luci.

"What'd you say?"

"If the name fits, wear it!"

"It's because of you I'm in here. Why don't you come in this cell and face me? We'll see how cool you are then."

With the inflection of Ole Scratch: "Sounds like yer lookin' fer two-fisted trouble."

"I'm incarcerated for sixty years and you're out there dancing?"

As if on cue, the janitor spun into a pirouette and quickly broke off into a rigadoon. He stopped with a "rata-tat-tat" and held out both arms.

"Haven't you done enough? You've ruined me."

"Cheer up, buddy boy. I gave you life, so to speak." Before Theo could utter another word, the janitor reached into the pouch on the front of his overalls and pulled out two bottles. "Barbeque?"

"You've got to be kidding."

"Wet or dry?"

Theo was dumbfounded.

"Come on, Theodore," the floorsweep uttered in Luci's voice. "I'm immortal and even I don't have your sixty years to think it over. Quit stalling. Make a choice and be a man about it."

Theo shrugged. "Dry rub. Now what does this have to do—"

The janitor handed the smaller container of dry rub spices through the bars. Before Theo could so much as look at the label to see if it was his favorite, the handle of the mop issued a loud crack on the cement floor. To the astonishment of Theo it collapsed and expanded all at once to form a card table. The janitor then pulled a red-and-white checkered tablecloth from his front pocket and snapped it into place across the table. From the other front pocket an elongated serving plate emerged, which was placed on the tablecloth.

Theo began to get hungry.

The janitor reached into his overalls and pulled out a large slab of ribs that he laid on the table, unspun the lid on the sauce, layered half, tore off a rib, and began munching away.

The janitor's face was now besmeared in crimson sauce. "You look concerned, Theodore Winterbottom. Don't worry. I'll share."

Theo's mouth began salivating. He knew it had been fifty-two days since his last dry-rubbed slab. He kept track with notches by the mattress in his cell. They matched the days he had spent in the clink. *But who's counting*, he thought and almost laughed.

"Actually it's been fifty-three days," the janitor said through a soggy mouthful of pork.

He's inside my head, Theo contemplated. *I'm losing my—*

"*Mind* passing me the dry rub?"

With quivering hand Theo passed the dry rub through the bars. The janitor sprinkled some on and tore off another rib, but this time passed it to Theo who could not resist. Theo stepped backward, never taking his eyes off the man at the table, until his hamstrings bumped the mattress and he sat down. Theo's lips went to work on the rib. He gnawed on the bone in an almost canine way. It seemed like the best thing he had ever placed in his mouth. He did not speak again until the bone was denuded of its flesh. His next question sounded asinine to him given the situation. "So what name do you prefer?"

The janitor swiped off his cap. "Drum roll please. Memphistopheles! Happy to meet your acquaintance on a more formal basis."

"You're tactless."

"By gauche, by golly. Say it ain't so."

"Why did you come here? You got what you wanted. Here I sit."

The janitor stood up and leaned against the bars while below him a pile of bones was forming. "To be honest with you, Theodore, it's your wife. She's driving us all crazy down there. 'Pick up this—put that over there—the fire's too hot—the flames are too red.' You know the routine. She's trying to run the place. I'm always after a new soul, but that woman is ridiculous."

"Ha! Serves you right." Theo moved back toward Memphistopheles and reached out for another rib, which was quickly obliged. "What do you want me to do about it?"

Two poker chips appeared over the eyes of Memphistopheles and he said, "Wager?"

"A bet? For Mary's soul?"

"Don't look surprised. I'm the biggest gambler of them all. Think about it. My habit started with Eve and I won that bet in tidy fashion. I called it the Gamble in the Garden. I wagered God for Job's life and lost that one. That hurt. God told me we were even. I told him to talk to the hand. A few thousand years later I tried to make three bets with Jesus in the desert. He wouldn't have any of it. More recently I bet Hitler he couldn't take over the world. He said that would be easy so I told him, 'Oh yeah, bet you can't do it with a funny looking mustache.' You see how that turned out for him. In hell we make him shave every day. It kills him," Memphistopheles said.

"You're sick," Theo reminded.

"Hey, throw me a bone here."

And with that Theo tossed the rib he had just finished between the bars and into the pile on the table, unsure whether the statement intended a pun. "So you think I will take a bite out of the proverbial apple?"

"It was a pomegranate, actually," he retorted, which he produced from the front pouch, inspected, and tossed over his shoulder. "If I win you get Mary back. If you win, a lifetime supply of dry-rubbed ribs and Mary stays with me."

Theo reflected long and hard. Finally: "If I'm going to take a chance on having Mary back, the stakes for you have to be much higher. If I win, I get a slab a day for life *and* I get outta here *and* one of my poems gets nationally recognized. Deal?"

"You sound like an infomercial," Memphistopheles said in Yam's voice. "Now pick your poison."

"The game is poetry. One hour, one page, one poem. Best one wins," Theo proffered.

"You of all people are trying to tempt the tempter. You're in no prison—I mean position—to do that." Memphistopheles considered this challenge for a moment then spun into a whirling dervish and the contents of the table disappeared. "You got a deal. I'll write on this table and you write in there. No peeking and may the best poet win."

On the table appeared two sheets of paper and fine writing instruments clad in glistening silver. He gave one to Theo and Memphistopheles immediately went to work.

Theo tried the pen and it was dry as Death Valley in the summer. "Hey, my pen doesn't—"

"Fifty-nine minutes and ten seconds left," Memphistopheles informed as he glanced at the Rolex. "Hope you don't get writer's block, Theodore!"

Just that very statement threw the fledgling poet into a tizzy. Theo's mind thudded to a halt and he forgot the poem he had been kicking around over the last couple weeks (a pseudo iambic pentameter about the turns of the Mississippi river mirroring the life of a disturbed teenage girl).

Memphistopheles wrote and wrote with passion and purpose, the likes of which Theo had never seen. And as he did, poor Theo resorted to pacing in a futile effort to unloose a poem of merit from the depths of his confused brain. Before Theo knew it, Memphistopheles slammed down his pen and raised the paper he had been writing on.

"It is finished!" The colorful man squirted off into a new dance resembling a peacock. When he finally came to a halt, he said, "Looks like you've never seen the Pavon before, Theo. It's an ancient dance. Learned it from the fine people at Paon. Those little strutters."

Memphistopheles glanced at the empty paper in the cell. "Not even a first word? Say it ain't so, Theo. To show you that I am not as bad as everyone makes me out to be, I'll give you the first word for free."

Theo looked through stabbing tendrils of hair.

"'The.' How'bout that for a first word?"

Theo cringed and just shook his head.

Memphistopheles checked the Rolex and espoused the latest time. "Hoom. Forty-one minutes and twelve seconds left and all is not well-ell."

"Pipe down," Theo said. The tick-tocking seemed loud as thunderbolts. For a moment Theo wondered if he was going to faint.

"I'll keep my words to a minimum," Memphistopheles assured, "just like your poem." He immediately took the opportunity to drag a bone from the pile back and forth across the bars in a rhythmic clanking.

"Would you mind?" Theo asked.

Memphistopheles broke into a round of foot tapping that transitioned into a tap dance impeccable enough to make Fred Astaire weep in his grave. All the while the watch ticked away. A few minutes later another bone appeared and Memphistopheles began playing xylophone on the steel bars. Theo vaguely recognized the song as *(I Can't Get No) Satisfaction* by the Rolling Stones.

It was in the middle of this commotion that a spark of an idea came to Theo from the serpent embroidered on Memphistopheles's ball cap. Theo swiped another pen off the table, with a confident air the likes of which Memphistopheles had rarely seen in his presence. This pen worked and Theo began to write.

"Ooh some action." In the voice of Ole Scratch: "That's what I likes to see."

Theo wrote and wrote as Memphistopheles called out the time with increasing frequency. In between he referred to Theo as "Theodork," "Theobore," "Theosnor," etc.

Memphistopheles danced and cavorted. He started repeating every derogatory statement Mary had said to Theo (in order and in her tone of voice), starting with, "I'm divorcing you."

When Theo stopped to think, he would clamp hands over his ears to drown out the noise. A minute later he began the next quatrain. This pattern repeated itself for a number of minutes until,

"Five seconds . . . four . . . three . . . two . . . one. Time!" And at that moment Theo dotted the last period. His legs felt weak and he slunk down onto the cold slab floor.

Memphistopheles was jumping up and down. "Let's swap and compare. Oh boy, oh boy!"

"Your poem first," Theo demanded. "Hand it over."

Memphistopheles complied. Theo scooted back against the cinderblock wall and read.

Mélange
By
Memphistopheles

The triumph He for us acquired.
 He cometh, Hell to extirpate,
Whom He, by dying, wellnigh kill'd;
 He shall pronounce her fearful fate
Hark! Now the curse is straight fulfill'd.

Round him busily hewed and hammered
 Mallet huge and heavy axe;
Workmen laughed and sang and clamored;
 Whirred the wheels, that into rigging
Spun the shining flax!

I desire the berries,
 But, in the mist, I only scratch my hand on the thorns.
Probably, too, they are bitter.

But see, amid the mimic rout
 A crawling shape intrude!
A blood-red thing that writhes from out
 The scenic solitude!
It writhes!-it writhes!-with mortal pangs
 The mimes become its food,
And seraphs sob at vermin fangs
 In human gore imbued.

Memphistopheles did the Moonwalk outside the bars and gave himself high-fives as Theo pondered the stanzas. They made no sense. A few turns of phrase seemed *familiar*. In Theo's mind there was a certain tinge of acquaintance in those verses and the title was his biggest hint as the verses fell into place like dominos.

"You charlatan!" he blurted and sprang to his feet. "The first stanza is Goethe, 'Thoughts on Christ's Descent into Hell', the second . . . the second is Longfellow, 'The Building of the Long Ship' no, I mean 'Serpent', and the third stanza is Amy Lowell, if I'm not mistaken, from her poem 'The Tree of Scarlet Berries.' That one threw me for a moment. The last is my favorite. Edgar Allan Poe. 'The Conqueror Worm'. They are all are tied to you. The vainest of the vain. I should have known."

"Didn't say it had to be original," Memphistopheles informed in a sheepish way.

"That's cheating."

"I prefer the term 'poetical recycling' and I doubt you'll beat it, Theodore, but let's have a look-see just for kicks."

Theo handed his poem over.

The Riven Mantle
By
Theo Winterbottom

"Alas! you'll leave our woodland and your maiden bands, unhappy girl, to wander in your own despite to the cities of the Greeks." – *Argonautica*, Valerius Flaccus

Medea, my Medea, through wolds of love you float, ne'r a fuss,
Once, in a time long forgotten, in a land where thoughts were pure.
Medea, my Medea, Hecate cast her scorn on thee and dredged a moat between us,
Your Jason, as he pens this, caused it to be sure.

This cloak of sorrow Hecate forced me to wear,
Hard by the Mississippi you sought to tame.
This sable mantle bringing forth the unwanted stare,
Hangs round my languid neck in shame.

You turned love to industry, making light of my lack thereof,
This cloak Hecate gave me, this inescapable flowing skin;
Has caused a marriage of neglect and wonton love,
Which mantle is riven to me, ne'r to be removed again.

May your soul of hate be vanquished where it rests,
Be it Hecate's fury or my vengeance that caused your death.
This Jason, your Jason, is putting forgiveness to the test,
Let my riven mantle be accursed 'til my last breath.

Theo faced Memphistopheles. "Even you have to know when you've been beat! A deal is a deal."

Memphistopheles balled fists at his sides and began stamping up and down. His cheeks puffed and face turned crimson. Steam issued from his ears and the cap began spinning on his head. Memphistopheles folded the table back into the mop from whence it came and tucked it under one arm. He tipped his cap to Theo Winterbottom. "Why'd you have to go and be repentant? I hate that!"

And with those words Memphistopheles spun into a dervish that caused Theo to grab hold of the bars so he would not be thrown back against the cinderblock wall of his cell. For a few moments he struggled just to catch his breath in the face of it. He held on with all his might as his feet began to lift off the floor and his torso went horizontal.

This went on for over a minute until the first change Theo felt was the attenuation of the wind on his face, followed by the bars in his grasp turning *soft*. When Theo opened his eyes to see what had happened, he was still horizontal, but was clutching bed sheets . . . and they were not made of the sandpaperlike material of the federal penitentiary, but the 600 thread-count, Egyptian cotton sheets he remembered from home. Above him rotated a ceiling fan from which emanated a gentle breeze.

"Thank you God," he uttered and at once leaned down over the side of the bed and with his face looking down, "I mean, thank you Memphistopheles." He saw from the alarm clock on Mary's side of the bed (there was never one on his side because this would have been a wasted piece of electronics) that it was nearly lunchtime.

Theo pounced out of bed. He slipped on his robe, flung open the plantation shutters and greeted a sunny day in the upscale neighborhood. He got a chill remembering the muddy footprints and Mary's blood on the sheets. He gingerly folded back her side. To his delight he found no stain whatsoever. Out in the hall the footprints were gone and so was the chartreuse police tape.

As he put on his bathrobe, a funny thought struck him, *This never happened. Memphistopheles. Ole Scratch. Beliala. Yam's ivory-handled gun.* Theo leaned against the wall and slid down it under a roar of belly laughter. It all seemed so absurd to him now from his McMansion in Memphis suburbia. *Memphistopheles! What a name. The guy sure could dance!* A fresh wave of hilarity overcame Theo as he sat there on the marble tiles. He was laughing so hard that at first he didn't hear the doorbell rang. On the third chime it got his attention.

Theo struggled to his bare feet, cinched up the front of his robe beneath the overhang of his gut, and answered the front door.

A young man stood there with a rather long box in his arms. "Your slab of ribs, sir."

"I didn't order—"

The deliveryman seemed in a rush. "One ninety seven Hargrove Circle?"

"Yep."

"That's is the address on the order. Just sign here."

Theo scratched on the pad and shuttled the ribs inside. He was starving and certainly wasn't going to argue his way out of a free slab of ribs. On his way into the kitchen the deal he struck with Memphistopheles, about ribs for life, crossed his mind. *Maybe it* did *happen. My poem beat Memphistopheles's hands down.*

He plunked the box on the center island in the kitchen and tore open one end. Just before he extracted the foil-lined bag inside, the garage door began opening. Theo froze. A few moments later the door leading into the house flung open.

The din of pumps knocked down the hall. "I just can't believe it! Why? *Why*?" It was a sobbing Mary; eyeliner racing down her cheeks. She was near hysterics. Theo almost expected a scattering of bullet holes in her blouse.

"Mary? What's the matter?" he inquired, almost too sappy and innocently.

"Oh, Theo," Mary said as she threw her arms around his neck, "Mom died in her sleep last night. I just got the call at work and rushed home. The maid found her late this morning." Mary immediately pushed back from Theo. "Well don't just stand there. We've got to start making arrangements. Do something, Theo."

Thoughts of Memphistopheles crashed into reality. Mary was back and so was his former life. The whole thing had been a dream. Inside he was somehow glad to have Mary back. They could make this work—he *wanted* to make this work—especially now that Luci was out of the picture. And the ribs? *I must've ordered them yesterday before I nodded off with visions of redemption and "The Riven Mantle" flittering through my active imagination.*

At times like these, Theo started doing what he did best. Food would help him think. He spun toward the ribs and extracted the foil-wrapped slab. A note fell out of the package. It was handwritten.

My Dearest Theo Winterbottom,

Yeah, yeah, yeah, you got me on the poem, but you have to admit I did a fine job stringing those stanzas of poetry together. You know what they say, "The Memphistopheles is in the minutiae." Enjoy the ribs and try a little wet sauce now and again! Live a little, Theo.

And don't worry about the publication thing. I'll follow up on that whole popular poet stuff as soon as I finish my rumba dance lessons. The rumba is killer on the hips and no foxtrot, let me tell you.

You may have guessed that you're not the first poet to win a bet with me. Milton did it. Who knew the shyster was so good at shooting arrows? For his winnings he demanded personal interviews with me that took hours for "Paradise Lost." Always wanting a first person account. That was old Milty.

Guess you're wondering about Mary, too. Well, your poem got me thinking and deep down I have to believe you want her back the way things used to be. It's your mother-in-law's entire fault for turning her on you. But I couldn't just give Mary back with Luci still hanging around. She'll have a great support group down here. There's a ton of other lawyers she can hang out with.

So there you go. I did a swap. Hope you don't mind the little modification to our terms.

Double or nothing?

p.s. I like Memphis ribs so much I'm thinking about going into the BBQ business myself. I've got this idea for a new line called: "Lake o' Fire Sauce - Guaranteed to set your soul aflame!" Luci's going to help me trademark it.

MEMPHISTOPHELES AFTERWORD

"Memphistopheles" is the longest story in this collection and the only I included in the title of the book.

The title is what gave me the idea for the story instead of the other way around, which is how it usually works among writers. We get the story in place, decide what the essence is, and on the backend think of a catchy title to tie up the story in a nice little bow.

Of all the clever monikers given the devil through the ages, Mephistopheles and Beelzebub are my favorites. With the former, I only had to add one letter and the name was transformed to represent a fallen angel who spends his time in the various haunts of Memphis.

In backwards fashion, I began with this great title I had kicking around in my head, planted it in the fertile soil of the Deep South, fed it barbeque, watered it with poetry (a *pastiche* for that composed by the devil) and watched it grow into the story you have just read. "Memphistopheles" is one of my first short stories and I have revisited it off-and-on for the past decade.

Who knew the devil had a penchant for barbeque? And as for me, I prefer dry ribs over wet.

The Mailbox War

August 2, 2008

AT WHAT POINT my woodworking hobby turned into an unabashed passion I cannot say. When can anyone really discern when they cross the line between love and extremism? My obsession with "mailbox art" is not any stranger than other concentrated areas of woodworking. Some toil for hours on soapbox derby cars for their children. Numerous illustrated books have been published on this very narrow topic. I have never spent a second on a wooden car. Other woodworkers ply their hands at fashioning miniature wooden ships that fit in glass bottles or marionette puppets or mahogany chess pieces. It is their passion. Is my area of focus any more odd? Are they somehow greater artisans of the ancient craft of forming wood from God's state to Man's state?

Custom mailboxes are my passion, the essence of my being. I melt inside just thinking about it!

Form is subservient to function in my artwork. I have taken it to levels previously unknown. For days I could discourse on the best paints to use in mailbox construction, which happens to be a mix of oil and acrylics. I have discovered there is only one type of hinge that will let the mouth open slowly and smoothly. The hinge will never squeak or produce unsightly metal shavings. I also know that it can only be procured from one manufacturer in Poughkeepsie. The mouth lip should be formed at an 87° angle to prevent water ingress and the wearing away of paint. The best mailbox grommets are found in the automotive industry. I am intimate with the best post mounts and the season of the year when they go on sale.

As for the proper wood to employ, oak is the most plentiful for carving, but I am also known to use pine, mahogany, white beech, walnut, red cedar, and myrtlewood. For all but the most detailed work I use a standard issue M7 bayonet knife that I got in Vietnam. This great utility instrument works equally well for killing or carving. I've stuck to the later since my return from the war.

All my boxes have address numbers that are hand painted in reflective paint. There are no cheap plastic stick-ons in my creations. The intricacies of the flags I use for the sides of the mailboxes, and their perfect 90-degree rotations, are worthy of a dissertation in themselves. In the down position they never move past a straight horizontal line. When I drive past mailboxes with "droopy flags" as I call them, I just laugh.

In my estimation there is an exact science to proper mouth dimensions on mailboxes. Large size envelopes must fit inside just as well as standard envelopes so they do not have to be delivered to the door. The internal grooves on the bottom of the mailbox must be just the right height so a nine-by-six-inch book will stand on its side and incur no spine damage. The mouth closure latches are also of vital importance and should be formed of J-shaped thermoformed plastic with UV inhibitor.

If a mere one component of a mailbox is cheap or not of grand craftsmanship, in my view the entire mailbox is worthless. Another tidbit Sarge used to tell us Bushmasters: "No one member is any less important than the others. The combined parts make up the whole."

Standing here at the end of my driveway I will not disclose any more of my trade secrets. At my feet was the shattered remains of my greatest creation. As I stared at it I blinked away spots of fury. The veins were strumming in my neck. How could anyone have done this to my monument to Debbie? I was having trouble with coherent thought. I vowed to do what I had always done and that is to focus on Debbie.

I am able to tell you the exact day I focused my passion into the art of creating fantastic mailboxes; for the experience was divinely inspired. It was the day after Debbie's funeral. My wife had worked as a mail delivery person her entire career. Long before email and instant messages Debbie realized the importance of delivering mail to the residents of our rural county. Habitually she drove her Jeep across the rutted, bumpy dirt roads that wind through it. She got satisfaction out of delivering paychecks and love letters from other parts of the country. Debbie knew when photos were being mailed to grandparents and when new children's books had arrived. By way of countless little white envelopes she cared for the people of Flummox County—showers or shine, snow or sun.

I know it is cliché and her life was one of routine, but I loved her to no end.

Debbie and I attended Flummox High School. We married right after graduation in '67. We were both kids madly in love and full of altruistic plans to change the world. Our first was to make the summer of '67 our own summer of love and we made great strides in that direction until I got sent my draft papers.

It was the day after our honeymoon in the Pocono's. Debbie was crestfallen upon learning she had actually delivered the envelope.

She begged me not to go. "It's only an hour's drive up into Canada," she reminded. She talked about renting a small cabin on a remote lake for a few years until the war ended. We could fish when hungry and live off the small amount of money we had got for our wedding and high school graduations. I wouldn't have any part of that. My duty was to the country and if it wanted me to go fight the Yellowman, so be it.

I planted a sapling ash tree in the backyard just before I was shipped off. I told her as the tree would grow so would our love.

The army trained me as a Bushmaster. I was rushed through basic training and a few rounds of shooting practice. When I got to 'Nam my captain—a guy only a few months older—immediately deployed me on nondescript search missions with my platoon. I brought up the rear when we took off on zone-and-sweep patterns. Bushmasters they called us. Oh the jokes we came up with just from that name!

The hilarity stopped once our rolling shifts into the jungle began. I survived half a dozen ambushes in the first month. Kill or be killed. Gook or be Gooked. I somehow avoided countless landmines when others in the platoon weren't so lucky. There's nothing more terrible than getting sprayed with your friends' blood. It made getting dusted with Agent Orange a pleasant experience in comparison.

Less than a year later I was home on medical discharge and Debbie was waiting for me. It took her a month to let on that she had breast cancer. Debbie knew for six months. She didn't want to tell me for fear it would make my job harder in 'Nam. That was the kind of person Debbie was, always looking out for my best interest.

Because of my *condition* after returning I couldn't work a nine-to-five. Debbie was okay with that as long as I did my fair share around our small house. She had her job at the post office. I stayed home and took care of our modest surroundings. Most days I would piddle with my woodworking tools. I made shutters for the front of our small home and gingerbread lattice from my hungry scroll saw. My sander allowed me to put a new facing on our kitchen cabinets. In the late afternoons, in spite of my condition, I would do my best getting us a meal put together. In the evenings Debbie would return and I would have dinner ready. This was not the manliest of duties for a solider fresh from 'Nam, but I did for Debbie. She deserved as much.

After we spent an hour or two talking, Debbie would retire to our room and read in bed, or wretch in the bathroom from a new round of chemo. On her good days I would catch her reading about the history of the U.S. Postal Service. She was especially fond of the first Roman mail service established by Caesar Augustus and how it evolved through the years.

We all have our hobbies and interests. Debbie's lasted all of three months after my return. The cancer got the best of her on our one year wedding anniversary.

As homage to Debbie and her love for the mail system, the very day after her funeral, I took to my small woodworking setup I had constructed in my one car garage. I was strangely filled with a desire to *create*, not destroy; to build again. How does the body, the mind, the central nervous system with its charged synapses morph emotions into energy and energy into creativity? My new hobby was a way to self-medicate after the loss. I did not leave the tight confines of the garage until I had recreated the Pantheon in mailbox form. What greater symbol of ancient Rome and the postal service it created for the world? What greater tribute to Debbie than to form a mailbox out of this symbol and place it by the road for all to see? I restored The Pantheon to its former Roman glory, miniature piece by miniature piece. It became an enduring testament to her life.

The first part I completed was the dome for which I used a bowl blank to form its convex shape. I carved the dome from hoop pine and bored in its center a smooth aperture that served as the oculus of the Pantheon. It gave extra light to the box's interior when I retrieved the mail. To prevent the elements from entering the oculus, I spread a translucent piece of plastic across its opening and staked it on with wood glue. I even painted the interior of the cupola to exactly match the matrix concrete on the original. Next I built the main structure that was nothing more than an open-toped box with the main doorway cut into it. The four sides and floor were also glued in place. Then I turned to fashioning the portico, which consisted of pinewood, knowing that this relatively cheap wood is excellent for the required painting because rain would sit for long periods of time on the portico before drying out. I ensured I coated the pinewood in four heavy coats of gray. I attached the portico floor to the main structure and the keyhole plan-view shape of the building was complete. Finally I built the pointed roof of the portico. Instead of the Latin phrase M - AGRIPPA - L - F - COS - TER - TIVM - FECIT ("Marcus Agrippa, son of Lucius, Consul for the third time, built it"), I stenciled "FOR DEBBIE VALSTROY, THE LOVE OF MY LIFE" and formed the columns that support it. The columns were pine rods cut to exacting and identical lengths. Since there was no fluting on them, it saved me a bit of time. I needed every second to carve the non-traditional stiff-leaf on the necking of the caps. In comparison, the top and bottom apophyges were much less involved. I secured the Pantheon on the existing pole that sat at the end of our driveway after removing the old mailbox that was nothing more than a hollow half-cylinder that one sees repeated on every street in America.

As I completed the installation it occurred to me that this monument to Debbie would be accessed daily by one of her coworkers at the Postal Service.

I took great satisfaction in this wooden monument of Agrippa's Pantheon. The work of art was the greatest thing I had ever created. It was written up in the local rag next to a large picture of me standing by the mailbox. This kicked off my little custom mailbox business. I have now made over forty mailboxes for various people in Flummox County. I have fashioned everything from an apple for a schoolteacher, to a striped zebra for a retired zoologist. A mailbox a month is a welcomed supplement to my veterans' benefits, social security payments, and spousal benefits under the small pension that Debbie receives from the U.S. Postal Service.

Standing there in remembrance of all these fond details of my life with Debbie (and afterlife as she has rested in peace a decade now), I opened my eyes and pretended that I once again didn't see the smashed Pantheon that lay at my feet. The mailbox—what little was left of it—was staked at the end of my driveway beneath which ran a corrugated pipe that connected one side of the ditch to the other. My driveway was paved, but the rural street that fronted the house was not. I shut my eyes and unknowingly bit my lip until blood came. In my rage I lost track of time, but I do know I came out of the house to get the mail at three in the afternoon, which is my daily routine. Now the sun was fading in the west. How many cars had driven past me in my state of unmovable shock as I stood before the decimated artifact of my love?

I cursed the drunken, careless drivers that often take to the back roads. Floating before me in the languid waters of the ditch was a streak of gray paint and beige splinters that once was the Roman Pantheon I formed with my own hands and tools. A broken column leered at me from the drainpipe. The portico was unrecognizable. Strewn up the embankment were jagged chunks of wood. The dome of the Pantheon sat like a cockeyed gooks hat on top of the pole.

That's when it struck me that the pole on which the mailbox was mounted had no damage whatsoever. Closely I inspected the ground beneath the mailbox. There were no skid marks. I immediately ruled out the possibility of a car sideswiping the mailbox. It was the middle of summer. There was certainly no snow or ice to contend with on the dirt road. It had been at least three days since the last rain.

The mailbox had taken a direct hit; a clean swipe. I envisioned the side-view mirror of a high truck, which may have caught the mailbox on the way past. If this was the cause of the mess then how was the *entire* box smashed front-to-back? Lengthwise, the custom mailbox stretched nearly two feet. There was no vehicle on earth with a side view mirror that extended two feet out from the vehicle.

This brought to light my worst horror. The destruction of the Pantheon was from someone playing mailbox baseball. I will spare you the sports metaphors, there was no question a bat had been taken to my masterpiece and the Pantheon had fallen to ruin from one huge swing.

August 3, 2008

I spent the next morning in tears as I tried to repair the shattered testament to Debbie's life. Through the singular rear window in the back of the garage I could see the ash tree I planted for her, which was now thirty feet tall. A multitude of splintered pieces were laid before me on the worktable. For hours I tried to fit odd shapes and pointy wood artifacts together. I did not eat or so much as take a sip of water. The Pantheon had to be repaired; it *had* to be.

The smell of glue and anger-tinged sweat was pervasive in the enclosed space of my one car garage.

Summertime was upon Flummox County and the closest thing to air conditioning was a small fan that sat buzzing on my table in the garage. I was used to it. This is what I did most days as I worked on my hobby, but today something had changed in me. The feeling was not one of newness and the sweet release of creativity.

Today it was drudgery. Today it was hurtful and the bad parts of my condition bubbled up inside me.

People around town call me a recluse. They hide their children from me and won't look me in the eye when I go into town for groceries. They don't understand the nature of my condition. I see them pointing out the windows at my house as they drive by. None of them live far from it. Nobody in Flummox County lives far from the house!

I just keep to myself. It's best for everyone. I don't bother them. They don't bother me, *until now.*

I glanced at the clock on the wall then down at the table. After ten hours the mailbox did not appear much better than when I brought it in pieces into the garage. I whipped a column against the wall. The glue, nails and binding clips were useless. The structure was impossibly broken.

I focused on the few readable letters that still existed from my carving: FOR DEBBIE VALSTROY, THE LOVE OF MY LIFE. As my vision wavered in anger I noticed that what remained of the letters now spelled the call-to-action words DE   STORY, THE   M. I gathered the letters up and tacked them to the pegboard so I could read them over and over. "Bok-Bok," I whispered to myself. "Bok-Bok."

In one heaving motion I swept the splintered wooden pieces off the table. They crashed onto the cement floor in a heap.

August 10, 2008

Over the next week I built an even more elaborate mailbox, stopping only for a couple hours of sleep most nights. I even ate in the garage, living off peanut butter crackers and water. I knew this bland diet would not distract me from building an even greater monument to Debbie. I of course had my medication with me, but took it sporadically in my fervor.

The new mailbox began to take shape. I was fortunate in that I had enough supplies built up from the custom mail order business I had developed over the years. Slowly and with exacting precision, my second great mailbox creation, which stood taller than the Pantheon, took shape.

Big Ben, that great landmark of London and clock tower of Westminster Palace, began to rise from the shadows. I could think of no greater symbol of the British Empire. Like the Romans, the British Empire took the inner workings of postal delivery to new heights. I knew Debbie would be proud and was smiling as she looked down on me from heaven.

From my research I knew that Big Ben was actually the great bell of the clock. Still, like everyone else in the world, I called the clock Big Ben. As master of this world I took liberties where I could get them. But never in the construction of my artwork.

So there I was looking at *my* Big Ben in the garage. The clock mailbox lacked nothing from the original. The four clock faces were operational. They comprised white stained glass and black minute/hour hands. This had been the hardest, most exacting part of my efforts and it forced me to leave the garage.

I made a trip to a local craft store where I found the four white faces set in a tea table. I bought four battery operated wall clocks and plucked out the timing mechanisms for operation of the face hands. I located a bell in an old toy box of a Flummox County antique store and mounted it in the interior of the clock faces. For more authenticity, I rigged it so the bell would ring on the hour.

On the day I was to mount the new mailbox to the pole, I completed a much less artistic endeavor. I painted a cinderblock the color of an F-105 bomb. On its side I wrote in red paint: VIÊT CÔNG, HÃY COI CHUNG, which implored the Viet Cong to come over to the good side.

Next I mounted Big Ben on the post. It stood nearly six feet. Call it a tall and inviting challenge to the box smashers of a week ago; bait, if you will. If Big Ben survived the Blitz of the Nazi's in World War II, certainly mine would survive as a testament to Debbie.

Sundown.

At exactly 7:52 PM, I watched for signs of headlights coming from either direction. The street was clear. Hunched over, I carried the cinderblock in my arms as I stole down the driveway. I pulled open the mouth of the box, which opened just under the front clock face, and slid the cinderblock inside. This time any use of a bat on the mailbox would cost dearly.

August 12, 2008

For three nights I peered through the curtains of my living room window. This from a chair I had pulled up and furtively placed in a corner so the perpetrators could neither see me nor my shadow. My driveway is not long in comparison to those in most rural areas where land is plentiful. This enabled me to sit there and listen to the melodic sound of the mailbox bell as it chimed each hour: eight, nine, ten, eleven o'clock and midnight.

On the third night I must have fallen asleep in the chair near midnight. I was startled from sleep to the noise of the living room window shattering beside me. The cinderblock had made its return, not to the garage but into the house. My chair tipped over and glass shards glittered from my lap. I carefully brushed them off. The cinderblock sat there on the carpet. I ran into the hall and flung open the front door. By the time I made it to the driveway the car was speeding away. It was an older model and small like one you'd see jamming the streets of Hanoi. There was the driver and the passenger who had taken his bat to Big Ben. He was pumping the bat out the window in defiance. I could hear his jeering and laughing.

The car did not stop at the end of the road. It took a quick left onto the paved highway and was gone. I was hoping for the brake lights to come on so the license plate would be illuminated. Obviously a few alphanumeric characters would have given the police a short list of registered vehicles in Flummox County.

At the end of the driveway, in the sickly light of the August moon, were the smashed remains of Big Ben. Three of the clock faces were destroyed. The fourth rested below the torpid waters of the ditch, glowing ominously in the moonlight.

I bent over and took a piece of the tower. After visually inspecting it I held it up to my nose. There was no question the Viet Cong had been in the area. I could smell their tiger balm. Once a Bushmaster has smelt their scent, he will never forget it.

<u>August 13, 2008</u>

Early next morning I called 911. A squad car was sent over to survey the damage. The responding officers found me in the garage hovering over the pieces of Big Ben. Its repair was useless just like the Pantheon.

"Mailbox issues, Bob?" one of the officers asked.

"Look what they did to my masterpiece."

"There is no need to call 911 for a mailbox smashing. We need to keep the lines open for real emer—"

"This is my life!" I snapped. "Don't you think it's an emergency when the Viet Cong have infiltrated us."

"The Viet Cong, eh."

I went on to explain to the officer how they had busted the Pantheon to shreds and now Big Ben. I took him inside and showed him the cinderblock still lying on the carpet. I had yet to clean up the shards of glass streaking the carpet. There was simply no time given my haste to repair the clock tower of Westminster Palace.

"I like the newspaper you taped over the window," said an officer. He peeled back the curtains in the living room and glanced out at the denuded post at the end of the drive. "Why don't you try a brick encasement around the mailbox?"

"Are you kidding me? They'll just tip it over, bricks and all. Plus that's no way to show off a piece of art when it's bricked over and slopped with mortar."

"Fair enough. I know you take pride in them. What about a strong wire cage around it for protection? You know, something that's see-through."

"No more than Leonardo would stretch a wire mess across the Mona Lisa or Michelangelo cage the Pietà."

"I guess posts extending up from the ground to protect the mailbox from the swipe of a baseball bat is out of the question?"

I glared at the officers.

"We'll ask around town to see who's behind this. Maybe Derrick Elwell or one of the football players.

They get restless just before practice starts. Of course, it's only a guess."

The other officer jotted on his notepad, then said, "We'll send a few extra patrols down the roads tonight. Other mailboxes weren't hit. Usually these smashers have a spree and take out ten or more. Because yours are so elaborate I suppose they are keying on them. Keep your eyes out for anything suspicious and try to get the make of the car next time. You did say late model?"

I nodded in frustration.

The officers left shortly thereafter. As the squad car pulled out of the drive, I began preparing for the biggest battle of my life.

I began ironing my old Vietnam uniform.

August 27, 2008

For the next two weeks I did not shave. My lawn went untended, turning crispy brown in the August sun. For the next two weeks I did not received any mail due to lack of a mailbox on the pole. There was no time to visit even the grocery store for basic necessities or to refill my meds. The squad car came by once or twice and I pretended not to be home.

Deep in my sultry headquarters beneath the single light bulb that hangs overhead and the call-to-action words: DE STORY THE M, I constructed my most elaborate mailbox yet—*Statue de la Liberté*. It would be a symbol to the world of my liberation from the tyranny of the Viet Cong saboteurs and the freedom Debbie gave me after the war. The United States took the mail system, in the nineteenth century over its vast uninhabited western territory, to new levels of complexity; from Pony Express to our modern express-mail delivered in the bellies of planes.

I fashioned the mailbox from copper like the original by Frédéric Batholdi that stands as a shinning beacon majestically over the New York Harbor. I have never worked with the copper medium before and under normal circumstances would have found it difficult to shape. My anger, however, allowed me to force the thin metal sheets into submission by heavy blows of the M7's blunt handle and the occasional kiss of my fist.

I reached for my bottle of medication and it was empty. I tossed it over my shoulder and kept working, pausing only momentarily to look at the ash tree out back.

The flowing waves of Lady Liberty's dress were first as I got a feel for the copper. Next I formed her slender arms and the tableau in her hand. On the later is chiseled the date of the Declaration of Independence. Only I didn't inscribe JULY 4, 1776, but rather AUGUST 28, 2008, which stands in the annals of my life as the day of independence from mailbox tyranny. In her right hand I glued a battery-operated candle that I got from a Christmas box in the attic. Like the original, it was a symbol of enlightenment. I next formed the face of the statue, albeit nothing as intricate as the original. At certain angles it had the appearance of Debbie. Atop the Statue of Liberty's head rested the crown of seven spikes. On the original they represent the seven seas and their seven continents, but on my sculpture they were the seven months I spent under artillery fire in 'Nam.

The base of the mailbox was generally star-shaped to match the actual structure. A mouth was formed for receiving letters and magazines therein. This is where the genius of my plan came into play. On the base I affixed a coiled spring and tact welded it in place. Into the center of the vertical spring I inserted a rod that extended down the center of Lady Liberty and served as her skeletal backbone. The spring rose nearly to the waistline of Lady Liberty so that it would neither blow off in the worst of storms nor be detectable by passersby.

I smacked the statue upside the head. It rocked and snapped back into place with a quiver. I sat there for an hour laughing aloud, swaying the statue back and forth. My finest creation had become indestructible from swings of a baseball bat.

When I emerged from the garage daylight was at play. I was unsure of the day, but guessed it to be Friday or Saturday. Since the prior attacks had occurred on the weekends, I was in luck. Conspicuously I mounted the new creation for all to see at the end of driveway. The Statue of Liberty mailbox stood over six feet tall at the tip of the torch. Vehicles slowed as they passed to take a look at her, kids pointing out the back windows. The shiny bait had been set.

Femme Fatal de la Liberté!

Upon veil of dark I crawled through the crisp monkey grass all the way to the end of the driveway. My face was besmeared the color of night. Dog tags were around my neck. I wore my old camouflage uniform to resist detection by the Viet Cong. Clenched in my teeth was the M7 bayonet. At the end of the driveway I rolled into the ditch.

There I lay in wait, body partially submerged, a trickle of water moving past my ears, Lady Liberty shinning down.

Each rush of a vehicle overhead knocked my heart into overdrive. I heard the constant roar of those rice-burning Viet Cong engines as they passed. I felt the occasional stray rock sting my flesh as it found its way into the bunker. Mosquitoes buzzed on their way to spreading Yellow Death. Crickets and cicadas sang grating tunes. The F-105 Thunderchiefs tore through the sky. A rat or some other furry creature skittered across my chest.

Femme Fatal de la Liberté!

For hours on end I remained motionless listening to it all—feeling it all. A Bushmaster in the hole. Then I heard *it*.

At first it sounded like the thump of a Huey's rotors. I know them so well. On closer listen I heard the whine of the old model car that I saw a few weeks ago from the living room window. The sound was unmistakably familiar.

The car slowed and I began to hear voices as the passenger-side window came down. It all happened so fast. *Phftt*. A whiff of air.

Lady Liberty knocked to the horizontal. The tableau, the spiked crown bending near. My creation sprung back to vertical.

Just as I planned the Viet Cong fell out of window as his swinging momentum carried him forward. There was a muted thud as he landed on the side of the road and rolled down into my foxhole.

He was disoriented and the wind was knocked out of him. I easily jerked the baseball bat from his hands. "Bok-Bok!" I screamed.

I grabbed the gook by the collar. He was shaking his head and spit was flying out his thin lips. The muck was draining off him in slow tendrils. The cowardly destroyer of my art was defenseless. In the tremulous light I noticed that GREED was the embossed trademark on the bat before bringing it down on the gook's head.

I knew I had to act quickly. The winking glow of brake lights filled the air. The driver's indecision was evident as he contemplated whether to help his friend or speed off.

I grabbed the M7 and lunged from the ditch. The blade punctured the back tire. The driver realized what was happening. A spray of gravel ripped through my uniform and into my shins as the car tried to speed away. On three wheels its velocity was greatly attenuated, which enabled me to catch up to it without running.

I did the same to the back tire on the driver's side and after I pulled the kicking, screaming driver into the ditch, I did the same to him as the other.

The car was pulled into my garage where I dismantled it piece-by-piece over the following weeks. I incorporated most of the items into car-themed mailboxes that I sold in my mail order business. It is amazing how well stick shifts work as flags and glove compartments as mailboxes!

Since no damage was done to the car, there was no trace of it on the roadside. The bodies of the cowards were disposed of in the backyard in tidy plots beneath the ash tree. I covered the fresh dirt with leaves and grass just incase the nosy officers came snooping around.

Present Day

I would be a failure if that was the end to my story. In truth, I have related only the beginning. Within the year I moved out of Flummox County. My work of art at the end of the driveway was a big selling point.

My mail order business, the one with the custom designed carboxes for receiving letters, is thriving.

After all this you are probably wondering where I moved when I left Flummox County; to what state, etc. You must think, like all the know-it-all doctors, that I am dangerous because of my condition, especially when I do not take my meds. You probably even want to know the city and what street I moved to and the exact address. That is just what the Viet Cong want, too.

I have confessed to a murder in these pages. There have been others. Think you can catch me? You don't so much as know my name, Gook.

I will tell you only this: I live in a lonesome house on a back road somewhere in the United States. On dark nights, when I get the urge, I wait in the ditch for the Viet Cong to try and damage my latest work of art.

One swing at my mailbox is all it takes.

I wait.

THE MAILBOX WAR AFTERWORD

I have always been fascinated by people who take hobbies to extremes after humble beginnings. Some begin by diving off the edge of the pool. The diving board is next, then the platform at greater and greater heights, only to try a tandem parachute jump, next a solo parachute jump and finally move on to base jumping. Others take the childhood enjoyment of collecting thimbles or candy dispensers and turn it into a lifelong passion where they amass thousands in adulthood. In my view all fiction authors began writing as a hobby and those with true obsession, talent (in some cases), and lots of good fortune turn it into a career, but that is a whole topic unto itself.

The protagonist in this tale is no different with his mailbox art. Only in this case it turns into a deadly obsession. At the heart of this story is that unpretentious, primarily utilitarian creation of mankind called the mailbox. What's sad about the whole thing is they tell us the U.S. Postal Service may be cutting back on its delivery days and that email and social networking sites may prove the end of the mailbox. Its very name conjures images of the oblong and boring, of the utilitarian. I imagined what would happen if one were to cross the obsessive hobbyist with this prominent house fixture (and very functional item) for receiving and sending physical mail. I spent most of my childhood living on dirt roads where my parents' mailbox was no stranger to swings of a baseball bat in the middle of the night.

Decades later Kyra and I were driving along a country road that skirts the Tennessee-Mississippi state line. We began noticing dozens of amazing contraptions to protect the mailboxes from baseball bat drive bys; each was unique and creative in its own right. On a sunny afternoon we drove slowly down the road and Kyra captured many of them in the collage shown on the front cover. Mix these protective lengths with art and a guy with a "condition," and dump it out on the ground. What you get is "The Mailbox War."

The Serpent and the Sepulcher

In a gothic city of the dead,
Mind brimming with dread;
On fresh soil did I mourn,
In ashen dress tattered, *torn*.

Hard by the tomb of my love,
Moonlight festering above.
Hands caressing the sepulcher of my loss,
About my soul this heavy, albatross.
heavy

When angry voices evoked a chilling pause,
I searched for them who thought I the cause.
In the distance macabre shadows danced,
Where heated passions and torches pranced.

Near the cathedral that once served our vows,
To my love I whispered: "Press lips once more to my brow."
But the dank air gave no consolation,
In the graveyard of a forgotten general who defended the nation.

Voices clamoring for me started to advance,
If I were captured there would be no second chance.
I fell prostrate at the sepulcher, cold and ghoulish,
Realizing persons of sanity would think me foolish.

In this deathyard of visible crypts;
Where corpses lie above earth and phantoms fly about cross tips.

How long had they sought me in the forest of hanging moss,
While I waited for opportunity to visit my newly lost?

A murmuring voice answered with bite,
"Merely count the moons since thy love departed—a fortnight."
"Who is there?" I cried, eyes searching across the tombs,
While in the distance steeple bells pealed a dozen haunted tunes.

The murmuring issued no-no, above,
from beyond the depths,
Floating on westward zephyr the remnants of my love.
"Are you one who seeks me, perhaps god or ghost;
Do you mock me, who loved him most?

Reveal yourself in this abode of stygian mores."
Suddenly a dark glimmer showed 'round a statue of forgotten lores,
A coiled serpent revealed itself. I demanded a name.
"I am not your concern, only shame."

"Shame? You ancient beast of woe.
Cursed forevermore and trampled under toe.
It's no business of yours being so bold."
"This from you, woman, who just lost your soul."

"Away with your forked tongue.
Leave me in this state of anguish I've become."
"If you desire me to leave, I will depart,
Never revealing the murderer of him who had your heart."

"In my state of confusion, beast of woe,
Tell me if you are friend or foe."
"Woman, I am your friend and very special."
"Ask me the truth you seek and I'll be your oracle.
Be quick now with a response,
Or you'll hear no more of my parlance."

"First tell me of the chiseled goddess on which you rest."
Hissed the response: "Doloresssss."
"You know mythology, I'll give you that and nothing more.
Now be gone from this graveyard by the swinging iron door."

"As you wish," the beast spat through glowing fangs.
"And you will never know the murderer who serves your pain.
I'll disappear in this funereal gloom."
My heart cried: "No please, I beg you, tell me why and whom.

When I saw his pallid body lying on the floor it gave me pause.
There was no evidence of the cause."
"The method was poison from the Belladonna plant.
Its memory has tried to leave your tortured mind but can't."

"In this city of runic palaces, disclose the killer, dark beast;
So I can possess a modicum of peace.
My heavy heart makes it hard to breathe."
"Learn now of the killer and begin to seethe.

If you must know the origin, need I say a word?
Look at your hands, woman, and all will be heard."
They quavered under moonlight as bravery I feigned.
Marring my fingertips was a deep scarlet stain.

"You're wrong," I burst in disbelief. "No blood was shed;
From tip of his feet to crown of his head."
The burnished beast was now a scarf 'round Dolores's neck,
It undulated a response with jab and peck.

"Blood it is not, or the answer is moot.
On your hands lingers the sap of Belladonna root.
That employed aptly in a Parthian war,
Against Antonius when it settled the score."

"What should I know of a strange plant used in rage?
Then you speak to me of wars from a primordial age.
I have no time for you and your tales of morass.
My love lies here, dead from what you claim was placed in his glass."

"You assert you were not the cause.
Yet my answer gives you pause."
"I despise your Belladonna discourse or even little blurb."
The serpent stretched close and whispered: "Call it the devil's herb."

"Spiteful lexicographer, oh tool of Hades, slither away!
Be gone Garden reptile. Appear not 'til light of day."
"I beguiled Eve, this is true,
Yet point no finger toward me for this wretched rue."

I clapped blemished hands to spinning head,
In futile effort to block those sounds filling me with dread.
With auditory cut and dash,
The serpent had revealed my dark and recent past.

It then formed a noose about Dolores's neck and began,
To tell more of the truth from which I ran.
"Perhaps your mind has blocked this trauma,
Of jealous rage that became a killing drama."

I looked away toward the sepulcher,
"Nonchalantly you reveal what caused him to inter.
This 'killing drama' as you so claim,
Transformed my life of promise to one of disdain.
In my defense, I found a note but a year after matrimony.
In his dresser that belied fidelity.
Bellicose I became, brimming in wrath,
And vowed to do away with him by a natural path.

In dark remembrance I now confess."
"You killed him, woman, after learning of his mistressss.
This act of malevolence became your only feature."
"Stop punishing me with your dark talk, cursed creature.
I have paid my price.

For just one moment enter the realm of nice.
My actions have left me permanently forlorn,
From that spring night when our young love was shorn."

The serpent inquired: "Tell me more of the note.
Of which your endearing heart it did smote."
"The contents are no business of yours; yet you seem to know all,
Use your clarity, beast, which you possessed at man's fall."

"I like you, woman, so I'll reveal,
Key points in the note and how it made you feel."
The serpent circled into a necklet,
Then down hewn forearm to become a spiraled bracelet.
"I see the words 'jewelry' and 'flowers',
Surely these items are not without their powers."

"These gifts are seared in my mind,
His love did they unbind.
Tell me something I do not know,
Or finally take leave from this ghastly courtroom show."

Hissed the beast: "Your investigative skills are poor.
Reach into your pocket and read it once more.
If you need from me that which is new,
Read carefully who the letter is addresssed to."

Unfolding the tear-stained note from within my dress,
I squinted at the name scrawled on the address.
"I demand, oh beast, you reveal the location of this 'Mrs. Tate'
So I may embrace the darkness and unleash my hate."

The reptilian snickered. "The simplest answer I will give,
She is a planner of events and therefore should live.
Jealousy did veil your eyes,
From seeing truth behind your husband's beautiful surprise.

A party was planned on your first anniversary.

This 'Mrs. Tate' is in no way an adversary."
My choking grasp fell short of the serpent.
To which it responded: "Repent, repent, repent.

Your husband's killing was all for naught.
He cherished your wedding vows newly wrought.
Now the poisoning sealed your wyrd.
You're one beat away from hell's forever pyre."

Closer now I heard the chanting,
Of searchers, angry and ranting.
Toward the hewn goddess I implored: "Help me escape their glare."
Yet the beast of hell was no longer there.

Dolores was free of her slipknot.
And me the horrid despot.
I wished it gone forevermore,
Never to darken my guilt-ridden door.

Suddenly I saw it twisting in spite,
Fangs bared and glistening in the moonlit night.
On the veined granite it now writhed,
Above my love who once teamed with life.

Its glistening tail pointed to carven stone,
Reminding me on earth I was alone.
I saw my love's deathdate—FIRST OF MAY,
"The enabling time of Belladonna, woman, the day of all days."
Then the beast snapped at me,
I started to flee.
I could hear them yelling in the crowd.
Their voices livid, loud.

Through the deathyard I scurried post-haste,
Skirting aboveground mausoleums with no time to waste.
At once Janus's wrought iron gate I did see,
And tore from that place with serpent churning after me.

Battered shoes carried me through murk,

While right behind me the snapping creature did lurk,
And voices echoed all around,
Until the familiar citadel of hanging moss I found.

Legs driving, fallen branches popping,
Arms pumping, branches whipping;
Darting, Darting,
Scampering,
In my chest a heart jackhammering.

I ran far from that deathly stygian more,
Help from God did I implore.
Shunning me He issued no reply,
—a lunar body as my only guide.
And
I
fell
to
earth.

There I lay in bruised and abraded heap,
My vows having failed to keep.
For hours on end weeping, weeping,
Until my weary head entered guarded sleeping.

Next morning with headache I awoke,
Lying beneath tree of stolid oak.
Next to bent and purplish hedge,
Its fruit the devil's job to rent and dredge.

I realized, as confused mind started to swirl,
Belladonna is the beautiful lady of this verdant wold.
The real mistress whom I sought.
She stole my love and killed him for naught.

S*he* enchanted on the First of May,
Then and there I believed in that light of rising day.
"'Twas all a dream," I laughed and shouted.
"He is still alive. I should have never doubted.

A nightmare I've had in this land of fays.
Where filtering sunlight announces hope of glorious new days.
Pshaw to sepulchers and talking serpents run amok;
And my fingertips they are merely stained with red muck."

I stood and exclaimed: "It's all been a cruel joke of Nyx."
When a glint caught my eye among groundcover of sticks.
Where my bespattered shoes lay off to the side,
And from them a particular glare I could not deny.

Slowly I picked one up for inspection,
It transformed thoughts to reflection.
This was neither comedy of night nor of Nyx;
In my shoe heel did two dreadful fangs affix.

THE SERPENT AND THE SEPULCHER AFTERWORD

This is the only standalone poem in the collection. I placed it right in the middle of the stories to serve as poetical backbone. It is hard to get most people to read poetry. It will come as no surprise that this is not a new phenomena in the literary world. In the mid-nineteenth century Richard Horne began offering his epic poem "Orion" for a farthing "to show his appreciation of the low esteem into which heroic poetry had fallen." The epic poem sold well, but fell out of publication in 1928. Eighty years later I compiled and edited a new edition complete with Edgar Allan Poe's glowing review of the poem. The new edition of "Orion" has not been a best seller by any stretch, and the low esteem for heroic poetry that Richard Horne alluded to still exists today. But it does not stop at heroic poetry. Few people, outside of academia proper read poetry for pleasure.

In an effort to change this I made The Serpent and the Sepulcher story-driven. My impetuous for the prose poem came after reading "The Raven." Poe's poem is very monochromatic in nature, a snapshot of a lost love names Lenore that will return nevermore. It leaves many questions unanswered. We do not know what happened to Lenore. Poe left us wondering where the setting takes place. We do not know how long Lenore has been departed, nor if she was married. We do not even know the name of the protagonist.

Edgar Allan Poe asserted that the most melancholy of all poetic topics is the death of a beautiful woman. I disagree. The ultimate poetic melancholy takes the split shape of a serpent's tongue. The most melancholy of all poetic topics is the death of a true love—beauty being in the eye of the lover—never to return. But that is only the "nevermore" prong of the forked melancholy tongue. To hear the deepest hiss of a lover's death the protagonist must have been the one who *caused* it. This is the highest melancholy of the poetic form: the death of love and its causation. Finality *and* guilt. A true love never to return because of the actions of the other.

It is this dual case of melancholy presented in "The Serpent and the Sepulcher." "The Raven" only gives us the first prong. Now the creature is no longer monotone. It does more than just sit on the head of a mythological statue and utter a dower word. The serpentine creature interacts with the statute through movement and the lady through hissing speech, ultimately divulging the cause of the lover's death and finally chasing the woman through the dark forest. The expired beautiful lover is no longer limited to a woman as Poe claims, but has become a man.

The Brownie of the Alabaster Mansion

Some thought he was a mongrel . . . some a kelpie, or a fairy, but most of all, that he was really and truly a Brownie.

The Brownie of the Black Haggs
James Hogg

I. The Tarwicks

BOOKER TARWICK OPENED one of the tall front doors on the ground floor of the Alabaster Mansion and stepped into a massive foyer overhung with an equally massive glass chandelier. A set of stairs flanked each side of the foyer and upon strolling through it he was met with a long hallway running perpendicular. Its oaken floor stretched down to the western wing on one end and the eastern wing on the other. Off the hallway sat a library where Booker Tarwick often worked from home. This evening would be no exception.

He had lodged a full day at Tarwick Timber Corporation and had another hour, maybe two, of calls to return. Being third generation CEO of the conglomerate demanded as much, especially when utilities were considering wood once more as a "renewable" fuel.

On his way down the long hallway he passed the map room, the china room, the room of gilded silver decorations that had yet to be named by Chelsea, the elliptical room leading onto the south portico (the most talked about room by the select few residents of the county who had visited it), and the parlor where the girls were camped out.

"Not so fast, Daddy," said Claire the towheaded eight-year-old.

Booker stopped dead in his tracks. He had been caught once again trying to sneak by. Claire was arranging a wooden chair while her three-year-old sister, Jan, had taken to running with a toy bus around the room.

"What problems of the world are you solving today? A new dance move? A new castle for the princesses?" As the father of two young girls, Booker was well versed in the latest princesses and teeny bopper dance moves.

"We need to know on which side of the fireplace to put the brownie's chair."

"A what?"

"A brownieeee, Daddy." Claire pointed to a book splayed open on the floor. "Says here in 'The Old Scottish Book of Fairies and Mischievous Creatures' Mommy gave me that if you put a chair out for a brownie he will come live in your house."

Booker Tarwick was befuddled. The girls' imaginations had no bounds.

Jan burst out with another passing of the bus around the parlor. "Airybus!" she exclaimed, running the two words together.

"Well?" Claire asked.

"Oh, the chair. I don't think, honey, it will matter to the brownie what side of the fireplace he sits on. Whatever a brownie is."

"Okay, Daddy, I'll leave it where it is."

Booker spun out of the parlor with a smile on his face. He had to get back to being CEO. The trust fund handed down to Booker Tarwick by his parents—the Timber barons Percy and Martha of Tarwick Timber Corporation, and before that his grandparents, Winston and Aubrey Tarwick—was every bit as generous as had been rumored in the county at afternoon teas, under church awnings and knitting clubs.

By the simple bequeath the young Tarwicks had become far richer than anyone in the county could imagine given the size of their intangible assets. Booker did not rest on his wealth. He had more than tripled the trust over the years due in large part to his love of innovation and a good, old fashioned work ethic that stuffed the coffers of his bank account and gave a tidy lifestyle to a few stockbrokers in Manhattan and bankers in Dallas.

Despite the constant media attention, Booker and Chelsea remained humble in the face of their fortune. They never stooped so low as to mention their money at any social function. They turned out to be religious and giving people. Their magnificent gifts to church and charity alike were all given anonymously.

There was one tangible asset, however, that could never be hidden from public view and that was their house. Of course to call it merely a "house" was to deem the Empire State Building just an "office building" or Route 66 a "road." Since Booker took over the mansion from his parents eight years ago, and decades earlier when his grandparents built the whitewashed bulwark of brick and stone over a five year period in the nineteen thirties, it had simply been known in the county as the Alabaster Mansion. This was due in no small part to its columned balconies and semicircle porticos lined with countless windows, each guarded by the finest wooden shutters and black iron hinges.

At three ample stories with peaked roofline, the venerable structure loomed over any house in the county. Its height, no matter how impressive, was overcome by the girth of the mansion that had expanded over the years by the addition of rooms, halls that began to form cohesive wings truncating in both east and west directions. The main residence sat firmly in the middle and was the oldest structure of them all.

The most recent addition was a multi-vehicle garage housing the many cars Booker Tarwick had collected over the years, including a 1928 Rolls Royce, a 1948 Cadillac Convertible Coupe, a 1940 Buick Super Touring Sedan and Booker's favorite, a 1936 Buick Three Window Business Coupe. Very few were his "driving" cars. They mostly sat beneath tarps and canvases on highly polished floors.

Above the ground floor was the stately floor of the Alabaster Mansion. It had many colorful rooms that Chelsea Tarwick had named accordingly; not liking the names Martha had chosen decades ago and those Aubrey Tarwick picked originally. A balcony overlooked the foyer and was adjoined on one side by a media room and on the other by the formal dining room that got most of its use at holidays and special gatherings.

The third floor held the main living quarters of Booker and Chelsea, along with their two daughters. Although the floor was large enough to have separate bedrooms for the gentleman and lady of the house, they slept in one and let the girls have their own separate rooms. Each bedroom had a sitting room, dressing room, one or two sitting halls off the dressing room, and a closet that in most houses in the county would have been called a room unto itself. The rooms were festooned in the finest linen draperies; walls hung in tapestries and family portraits by popular artists. An elliptical room overlooked the pool, gardens, tennis and basketball courts of the backyard.

All floors had multiple fireplaces inset with ponderous andirons and were overhung by carven mantles and family portraits going back to Winston and Aubrey Tarwick.

Being patriotic, Booker named the guest bedroom after a famous president. As a natural extension of this patriotism, it was no secret in the county that he was a man of conviction and high-minded principles. Although the situ of the Alabaster Mansion was in one of the wealthiest counties of the region, there were certain pockets of poverty. The family had always been generous in their charitable giving to deserving families. Yet there are many in the county who felt they should give all their wealth away to the poor, even if they were lazy and did nothing to help themselves or others.

Combined with his rather bullheaded way of getting his point across, Booker was looked down upon for never compromising in his many ultimatums issued from an impossibly long table in the boardroom of Tarwick Timber Corporation or the mahogany library of the Alabaster Mansion. This was especially true amongst leaders in the county who, if truth be told, wanted him and his family, with their anti-environment business and high-minded values, to leave the Alabaster Mansion for good. This attitude was only exacerbated when Tarwick Timber Corp. began having financial difficulties. The buyers for the company ran up huge deficits and the finance department lent money on very unfavorable terms. When key suppliers in the wood industry began filing for bankruptcy, the book value of Tarwick Timber Corp. sank. Booker was forced to lay off many workers. No department was unscathed.

The Board blamed Booker for lack of oversight and he blamed the Board.

II. A PECULIAR SPECTACLE

This weighed on Booker that particular late fall evening when he was making a few last phone calls of the day from the library. He heard a most peculiar sound in 6/8 metre that had never been heard on the grounds of the manse before despite the many social gatherings held under its porticos on summer evenings. He flung open the drapes and stared outside where he noticed an odd jumble of people dancing and strutting up the winding driveway of the manse in the grandest of fashions. Booker had no idea how the party had made it through the gate that was always to remain locked without a passcode as they curved off the driveway and were making an arching path up the verdant lawn.

Leading the pack was a riding lawnmower team that at first did not strike Booker Tarwick as out of the ordinary. The acre upon acre of verdant lawns surrounding the Alabaster Mansion had to be maintained by a fleet of groundskeepers on a weekly basis. Yet what struck him as out of place was to see the group riding in *tandem*—synchronized mowing if you will—all dressed in coal black uniforms and perched on machines that matched.

Marching right behind the lawnmower brigade was a band—consisting of three violins, two guitars, two trumpets, and bass—playing in the mariachi style. Their music was difficult to hear over the rumble of the riding lawn mowers. The band wore wide-brimmed hats and gilded dark outfits. They all wore shiny black boots.

Behind them was a knot of ladies dressed like Scarlett O'Hara in her Sunday best. Their frilly gloved hands were holding signs that read FLOWER MATRONS. There were proudly kicking their legs out in front to reveal sable garters. Each held a pail in one hand from which they were throwing dark flower petals into the air.

At mid-lawn the group stopped, led by the riding lawnmower team, and parted right down the middle; the mowers looking back at the marching band, the band craned their instruments back toward the dancing ladies, and the southern belles extended their arms behind them to reveal the most bizarre person in the entire impromptu spectacle.

There was a wisp of a man bringing up the rear of bus, so to speak. He was dressed in a cheap pinstriped suit that flapped open below the lapels to reveal a crimson necktie. Above the tie a cigarette dangled from his mouth. There was a definite swagger in his walk as he made his way up the front lawn, hands cupping behind at each step. It struck Booker as more of a strut or sashay than a walk.

In the twilight, it was difficult to make out his facial features.

The little man stopped in the grass and flung both hands into the air. He began waving crazily as though the entire world loved him and were bursting with excitement at his arrival. Booker scanned the surrounding area but saw no one there except those in the parade. Booker noticed that the little narcissist did not quit waving until he had made a full turning circle.

At the dropping of his hands, the members of the parade filled in the center gap and marched another fifty yards to the front of the mansion. Just as Booker was about to call the police, the parade once again stopped and from its middle emerged a chunky preacher that had previously gone undetected by Booker Tarwick from his windowed position in the library. The timber magnet knew the man at the forefront to be a man of the cloth for no other reason than he held a large Bible in one hand.

The lawnmowers were shut off and he began to preach in a manner that did little to bring Booker closer to God, especially in his agitated stated. The short and peculiar sermon focused only on patterns and high fashion. It soon became evident that he was promoting only his style and hated all others.

The preacher's bizarre sermon ended in a flurry. "Let the polka dots rot. May the stripes be wiped. The herringbones shall be dethroned. Let the plaids die rad. May the minds of the paisleys turn lazy and may God deliver a wrecker for the checkers."

With that the lawnmowers revved and the band struck up their instruments. The parade curved back toward the driveway, which was to the west of the Alabaster Mansion, and when they reached the snaking driveway again—right at the point where they moved off it—they marched away in formation across the gravel-shot with the mowers spraying pebbles twenty feet in either direction. The previously immaculate lawn now looked horrible.

Booker Tarwick slammed his eyelids shut. He had clearly been working too hard of late. *I didn't just see that,* he reasoned as he clutched the draperies. *I was forced to sign those new executive guidelines. I didn't want to but I am a man of high principles.*

He took a few deep breaths, afraid to open his eyes. This was useless in blocking out the auditory whir of humming blades and high-pitched horns.

With one eye open, he saw that the parade was *almost* out of sight and with it the funny little man who brought up the back of the bus and for whom, apparently, the extravagance had been for in the first place.

III. In the Mansion

In the ground floor library, Booker Tarwick fell asleep in his studded leather chair. He had worked longer than anticipated. It was restless sleep as he mulled over the strange events that did—may—*did not*—happen on the front lawn. He had said nothing to Chelsea or the girls to prevent their alarm. Besides, he was increasingly unsure if it had all been a figment of his overworked imagination; a stain on a guilty mind for being handed wealth instead of having earned it no matter how well he had taken over the reigns of Tarwick Timber Corporation; a stain on a guilty mind for letting the company slip into financial difficulties over the last couple years.

"What about the O carved into the lawn?" asked a tiny voice. "The Big O."

Booker's mind was working overtime. He glanced over at the clock—8:37 P.M.

"And the noise?"

He tried to focus on anything but the events of twilight. He rotated from hip to hip. The leather chair gave off a squeak.

"Uh look at the flower petals on lawn. 'Black violas' is what they called them. Go touch one. *Touch it!*"

Shut up, Booker thought to himself or had he mumbled the response into the dark room? The agitating thoughts were coming through so clear now, as though someone was whispering to him from behind the chair.

"The flower of treachery, hee, hee, hee."

Okay, Booker Houston Tarwick the Third, lift head, clamp hands over ears, press on both sides (AAA batteries not included, but order in the next ten minutes and we'll double it. That's right! You'll get two Meaty® Hand Pillows for just $19.99. Shipping and handling not included. Act now!). Void where prohibited. Booker Houston Tarwick the Third Timber Corp. hereby disclaims all express and implied warranties, including the warranties of merchantability and fitness for a particular purpose. Use of the Meaty® Hand Pillows is done at the consumer's own risk and mental health. All *consumers agree to indemnify and save harmless Booker Houston Tarwick the Third Timber Corp., its officers, affiliates, agents, joint venture partners or representatives from and against all losses and all claims, demands, suits, actions, payments, judgments arising from personal injury or otherwise, brought or recovered against the Booker Houston Tarwick the Third Timber Corp., its officers, affiliates, agents, joint venture partners, or representatives by reason of any negligent act or omission of the Booker Houston Tarwick the Third Timber Corp., its affiliates, agents, joint venture partners, servants, or employees in the performance of this Contract including any and all expense, legal or otherwise, incurred by Booker Houston Tarwick the Third Timber Corp., its officers, agents, or representatives in the defense of any claim or suit . The consumer is responsible for paying all sales taxes to the appropriate governmental entity. All products are shipped F.O.B. side of head, freight prepaid and allowed. Title and risk of loss pass upon shipment to the consumer. The Booker Houston Tarwick the Third Timber Corp. warrants that the products provided hereunder will be new, free from hangnails in material or workmanship for the period of one day or twenty four hours, whichever occurs on the first gravel-shot—*

"Gravel-shot everywhere!" came the whisper.

It's all a trick of light. Every bit of it.

Booker extracted himself from the chair, moved slowly down the long hall and began climbing the stairs to the third floor. His head was pounding. Half way up he heard a high-pitched scream that was unmistakably Chelsea's. He raced up the steps.

When he reached the third floor he could tell the scream was coming from the master bedroom. By the time he reached the threshold, Chelsea was dashing out of the bathroom where she had been taking her nightly shower.

"In there," she cackled, pointing behind her with nothing but a towel on. "A little man in a suit."

Booker moved into the bathroom. He looked for a heavy object to defend himself, but in the large space the marble countertop, with its solid pewter soap dishes and bottles of fine perfume, was a good three steps away from the door.

He saw nothing out of the ordinary. He quickly scanned the framed oval mirrors over the sinks for a reflection of the man behind the door. Nothing. He looked at the massive shower that had showerheads directed at every part of the body and arched entrances on both sides. The water was still pulsing. A cloud of mist was pushing toward the high ceiling. With its slightly opaque glass walls, Booker was able to see if a person was inside it. Nothing. Same with the "commode closet" as they called it. He searched around the bottom of the claw foot tub and again came up empty.

Booker stepped back into the bedroom where he found his wife visibly shaken as she sat on the edge of their four poster bed. "All clear. There's no one in the bathroom."

"I swear I saw a man. . . or he saw *me*, rather. I was taking my shower when I noticed two beady eyes staring at me over the top of the wall. He must've been standing on the clothes hamper. The peeping tom was giggling."

"What did he look like?"

"I didn't get a good look at him before I ran out. He had big, round ears, cropped hair, beady eyes—"

Booker got to thinking. "What was he wearing? Can you remember that?"

"A suit. A cheap pinstriped suit and necktie. I already told you that, I think."

Booker let Chelsea know that it was safe and further that no one could have run out without one of them seeing the inquisitive fellow in the first place. And as he ratcheted down into this calming mode of one-sided conversation that every husband becomes versed in at some point in his marriage, Booker was thinking of the small hinged door that was cut into the back wall of one of the lower master bathroom cabinets, the one his grandfather told him about before he died in 1974 of kidney failure.

Like any manse expanded over the decades, it had secret doors and hidden passageways that led into rooms or onto one of the porticos that stood in columned splendor on the south side of the Alabaster Mansion. Chelsea didn't know about this particular one and Booker was certainly not about to let her in on the secret now. This included the strange events at twilight that were becoming more real by the moment.

Booker pulled on his silk pajamas. He too noticed something peculiar in regards to his nightclothes. The armpits of each shirt had apparently been sprayed with a dark liquid that made it appear he had been sweating profusely.

Booker held one up for Chelsea to view. "Would you look at this?"

Chelsea noticed but didn't notice. She was not convinced that it had all been in her brain as evidenced by her pinched brow. She made her way over to the dresser and slid out her undergarment drawer. It took but a few seconds for her to ask Booker, "Do you smell that?"

He took a deep breath. "Yeah, almost like rotten—"

"It's coming from my drawer." Chelsea reached down and took a whiff of one colorful panty after another. "They all smell like . . . fish!"

She immediately scooped them up in a large armful. As she did, a fetid sardine dropped out of the pile and thumped onto the bottom of the drawer, its dull eye lolling in its socket. Booker rushed over.

They both agreed the maids were to get a stern lecture in the morning. The family had always paid them well and treated them with respect. If the sardine embedding and armpit spraying was intentional, the whole lot of them was gone. Though the Tarwicks had always hired illegal immigrants to work in their home, in public they spoke out against those who did not have a working visa in order prior to entering the county from a bordering foreign county. Booker had gone so far as to offer to pay for a fence along the entire border, which angered many in the community.

While Chelsea pulled on her nightclothes, which consisted of flannel pajamas in the fall and winter months, they agreed they needed to get as far away from their bedroom as possible to calm their nerves. Chelsea suggested they grab a new book from down in the library. As they headed out of the bedroom, Booker pinched the sardine between his fingers and carried it with him.

All was quiet in the Alabaster Mansion, perhaps too quiet. They reached the ground floor and made their way down the long hall to the library. On their way past the parlor Chelsea noticed a pinpoint light winking in the darkness. She knew the security devices were attached to the windows and quickly ruled that out as a possibility. It occurred to her that one of the girls must have left a toy on in the room, perhaps a broken headlight on the bus Jan had become enthralled with of late. She grabbed her husband by the arm and flicked on the overheads.

Booker and Chelsea could not believe what they saw in the chair by the fireplace. A little man in a cheap suit sat there with his shoes propped up on the fireplace screen, drawing on a cigarette. On either side of his cropped black hair were set funny round ears that appeared to move as he puffed. Deep wrinkles formed a pair of parentheses at the sides of his thin set lips. It struck Booker that it could've been a math equation with a minus sign in it. A large mole—or perhaps wart—glowered from the side of his nose.

"Nice pad," he said.

"That's him! That's him!" exclaimed Chelsea. "He's the one who was looking at me in the shower."

At this the funny looking man raised his eyebrows and winked.

"Who are you" demanded Booker, "and what are you doing in our house?"

With this the man sitting next to the fire glow responded, "The better question is, 'Why are you . . . waving a fish . . . at me . . . in threatening manner?' Very Square."

Made conscious of the sardine, Booker tucked it behind his back. "I'll call the police," he warned, "if you do not leave our premises this minute."

"Chill, Daddy'O. Talking is always better . . . than acting. Nice silk threads."

Booker noticed the way the creature would stop every four or five words and pause. This broken staccato rhythm annoyed him to no end.

By this time the girls had heard the commotion and wandered downstairs in their pajamas rubbing sleep from their eyes. Claire stood next to her mom and Jan took a flanking position that peered through the legs of her father.

Claire began pointing. "What the book said really worked. It's our brownie!"

The last word got Booker thinking about colors and he realized that it was hard to know what color the brownie actually was. In the glow of the firelight his skin had tinges of brown, white and yellow, but yet he was very green. It was impossible to know the true color of this kaleidoscope creature. There was no way to pin a color on him.

"What's your name?" asked Booker in a terse voice.

The brownie responded with a long flurry of a name that none of the Tarwicks could understand. Phonetically, Jan probably came the closest. To Chelsea it sounded Middle Eastern. Everyone in the room felt embarrassed for him. It was almost as if he was ashamed of his real name.

The brownie took a drag and stared at his shoes.

"Let's pick our own name for him, Daddy."

Jan raised her little hand and emerged from her hiding place. "Me, me, me!"

"Okay, Jan, what do you want to name the brownie?"

The three-year-old looked at her yellow toy vehicle on the parlor floor and said, "Airybus!"

"Can we keep him, Daddy?" said Claire.

"We'll see."

"Pleeease! I wouldn't have invited the brownie over if you had let us have a pet."

Truth be known, the girls wanted a dog but first got a goldfish that lasted all of two days. The family compromised with a pet hamster that did the trick for a few weeks until Jan left the top off its hamster home and it was never found again much to the dismay of Chelsea.

"We need to learn more about him before we invite him to stay," Booker said. He was worried about immigration laws and getting busted for having an illegal alien working in the house. "Let's see your proof of citizenship with full name."

"Whoa, Daddy'O. I don't carry no birth certificate . . . on me."

"Fair enough. You'll need to answer some questions."

The brownie stood up from the chair, took a long drag, tossed the cigarette on the marble floor that surround the fireplace, and crushed it out beneath his shoe. He propped an elbow on the large fireplace mantle, exhaled a tributary of smoke, and said, "Bombs away." Immediately he waved his hand and let the family know he was only kidding. He did not appear to have a violent bone in his thin frame.

Before Booker or Chelsea was able to ask their first question, the girls began their inquiry. Claire wanted to know what about the brownie's favorite animal.

"Groovy. Donkey is my favorite animal. Fox is my least favorite. If there was one around I would pummel it; beat it right down to the ground with my bare fists. They are on my jive list. Don't care for the elephant much, either." Airybus then rambled on and on about his other favorite *torva bestia*. This brownie loved to talk, or at least to hear himself talk, and he also enjoyed looking in the parlor mirror while he did it.

Booker thought the brownie's choice of likes and dislikes in animals was directly opposite to his. He chalked this up to yet another in the growing list of strange events and ideas surrounding the new visitor in the Alabaster Mansion.

"Best nut?" asked little Jan.

At that, Airybus announced that the acorn was his favorite of all the many and varied nuts in the world.

Claire tugged on her father's silk pajamas and once again asked him, "Can we keep him?"

Booker looked over at Chelsea and shrugged. "Looks harmless enough."

"And he is funny looking," added Claire.

"I just don't know," said Chelsea.

Hearing that, the brownie made outlandish promises to every member of the Alabaster Mansion in the hopes they would let him stay. To Booker, Airybus offered to turn his company around single handedly, to start hiring all those he laid off, and on top of that, to employ personnel at no cost. Speaking to Chelsea, who still refused to make eye contact with him, the brownie promised her greater rights in the household to which she had never experienced. The girls were offered free sports lessons and admittance to any school of their choosing. Yes, they all became his special interest and were all confused as to how the creature was to perform such miracles.

But alas his stupendous promises found a home in the minds of the Tarwicks, built on a foundation of hope more than reality. It was Chelsea who turned back to the brownie and warned in a stern voice, “You may stay as long as you keep out of our room and the rooms of the girls. Got it?”

“Shar ‘nough, Lil Gurl. Or should I say ‘Big Gurl’ after what I saw in the bathroom?”

Chelsea nearly wretched at the comment and ran from the parlor.

Booker sternly warned the brownie that there was to be no smoking in the house and went to toss the fish he remembered he was holding.

IV. A New Home

Weeks passed as the Tarwicks got to know their new Brownie. As expected, he was mischievous in the grand style and tradition of those from Scottish and Irish lore. Practical jokes were foisted on the family at all hours of the day and night. They were harmless and the girls participated in many of them.

Booker spent his usual long hours at the office and had little interaction with the creature other than casual observance. Chelsea was sure to keep her distance from him. She frequently complained to Booker, when he arrived home, of the latest antics of Airybus. Booker maintained that he was harmless.

The girls loved their new playmate. When he was not in his chair by the fireplace munching on acorns, he was outside playing games with them and tugging away at a cigarette. Basketball was his favorite game. When the girls weren't around, he would break out a game of Around the World for he claimed people knew and loved him worldwide. Booker was astounded at the narcissistic nature of the funny-looking creature who did many things to anger the owners in his first few days in the Alabaster Mansion. He tried to change many things in the manse even if it meant excluding members of the family. One example was that Airybus would not let the girls play basketball with him. It was clear he enjoyed playing with himself, of which he was very adept, bouncing the ball at all hours of the night on the west side of the house. This infuriated Booker and Chelsea who heard the noise all the way up on the third floor bedroom.

The Tarwicks observed that golf was his other favorite sport. Many afternoons Airybus was spotted hacking away on the verdant lawns of the Alabaster Mansion—divot after divot, clumps of grass chunking into the air, dirt flying. The first Wednesday after he arrived, Airybus shanked a nine iron. The ball went crashing through a greenhouse window. Chelsea saw it all on one of the security monitors. A look of horror crept over the Brownie's face. Head bobbing, hips swaging, hands cupping out behind him, he strutted over to see the damage. When Airybus arrived at the outbuilding he was distraught to find the hole in the top of the outbuilding and immediately began covering it up. He was either trying to hide the damage or very concerned about greenhouse gases that might escape. To Chelsea it appeared to be the latter since he was trying to fit small pots in the hole.

The girls and Chelsea immediately ran out to survey the damage. They found the brownie cross-legged on the floor, acting more cool and mellow than ever, smoking herbs he had found in the greenhouse. They told their father as soon as he got home from work, as they knew smoking was bad and had been frequently reminded of this as Airybus flaunted his habit around the manse.

Booker stomped into the parlor where he found the brownie sitting in his chair, shoes on the grate. "I heard about the greenhouse," he informed. "I demand that you inform these little girls you did not inhale the herbs in the greenhouse today."

"Oh, I inhaled alright. t was fantastic. A little turn on, that's all. You got some fine herb . . . out in the greenhouse, Daddy'O. Real fine."

"You blackguard," Booker responded in distaste.

"That's salty. The pot had better not call this kettle black."

V. SMOKE

The financial problems at Tarwick Timber Corporation weighed heavily on Booker. His time at work extended into most weekends and when he got home, his time "finishing up odds and ends" in the library went late into the night.

Airybus, in his effort to help the dire state of Booker's company, had unilaterally hired not one, but two secretaries to help the CEO in his efforts at turning the storied company around. One had international experience and one domestic. They were hired at no cost (as promised). Booker at first was thankful for the gesture. After all, the brownie was staying in the manse for free.

When Booker first met the secretaries, he was shocked at the base ugliness of the big-haired secretaries. Crow's feet shot out from their squinty eyes, their cheeks sagged into the points of their pinched lips. A turkey's waddle had attached itself to their necks. They wore heavy makeup and rueful perfume that caused Booker to gag. This, of course, made Chelsea happy and she had no concerns with her husband staying up late working with the ladies. She admitted for the first time that the brownie had a few redeeming qualities.

On one particular evening, Chelsea wandered sleepily down to the first floor and into the library where she found Booker dictating notes to the secretaries who sat eagerly across from his desk with computers spread across their ample laps. It was ten minutes to midnight.

Above the click-clacking of keyboards he said, “Final notes to the Board. I promise.”

“When’s it going to end, Booker?” asked Chelsea. “This . . . this vicious cycle. The more you work the more you have to do.”

“I am almost finished with my last letter.”

“It’s not this one letter . . . or the next. You need to step back from it all. *We* need a vacation; just you, me and the girls.”

The Tarwicks owned a lake house in the Northeast that had served as a retreat for them for over two decades. When Chelsea wanted to take a restful vacation, Booker knew where they were heading.

Booker, a captain agreeing to take a rest while his ship was sinking into the abyss, asked one of the sea hags across from him to lock in the next commercial flight. He had stopped using the private jet of Tarwick Timber Corporation months ago, which pleased the shareholders for about a week until the stock began tanking once more. At that point there was talk among the members of the Board to remove Booker as chairperson. It was decided behind closed doors to allow him to complete his eight year tenure, which—per the bylaws—was the longest a person could serve as chair.

The following morning—crack of dawn—the household was awoken by the blaring sound of smoke detectors going off on the first floor. Booker was the first to make it down the two flights of stairs. He snatched a fire extinguisher off the wall in the laundry room and rushed down the long hallway to the parlor. He suspected that one of the girls or servants had closed the fireplace flue before the last of the embers had extinguished and that was why smoke had filled the parlor.

On reaching the entranceway his first response was that he was right. Along the timber-lined ceiling of the parlor were roiling clouds of smoke. He glanced at the fireplace and saw that it had not been used in days. The brownie's chair next to its dark, gaping mouth sat empty.

Booker dashed toward the windows that lined the opposite wall in an effort to get them open and reduce the wallowing smoke. Two steps and he was airborne. The brief journey was disorienting. His torso gyrated. The extinguisher knocked against his anklebone midair. He landed hard on his shoulder and rolled up against a table leg that got introduced to his spine in a less than desirable manner.

When his eyes blinked into focus he saw Airybus on all fours swatting at the area rug with a sofa pillow. A semicircular ring of smoldering carpet fanned out from the brownie. On the charred rug that remained between them, Booker noticed a cigarette that had been smoked halfway lying next to the handheld fire extinguisher. At that moment Booker realized two things: he had tripped over Airybus on his way to the windows and it was the creature's dropped cigarette that had caused the fire.

Booker reached out for the extinguisher, ripped out the safety pin and squeezed the handle. A spray of white chemicals fanned onto the area rug and across the cheap suit of the brownie who ejaculated, "Easy on the threads!"

Short of breath, Booker struggled to his feet and pushed up three of the windows. Airybus helped Booker drag the area rug out one of the back doors and into the yard as Chelsea and the girls watched from a distance. With ceiling fans whirling and windows full open, it would take them over an hour to clear the parlor of smoke.

By this time the firemen had come and gone, but not before giving the Tarwicks a stern warning about smoking in general and especially indoors. The police had also arrived, given the high profile of the Tarwicks in the county. When looking at the charred rug on the lawn, one of the officers noticed the brownie climbing in one of the windows Booker had opened in the back of the house. When the officer asked the brownie who he was and whether he had rights to be in the Alabaster Mansion, Airybus tore into a rage. His funny round ears morphed into a claret shade and the mole on the side of his nose began to glow. Standing in his cheap suit smeared with evaporating chemicals, Airybus called the officer all kinds of monikers ("stupid" being one of the nicer terms) just because the officer was doing his job and looking out for the owners' safety.

Once the girls were nestled back in their beds, Chelsea and Booker confronted their brownie in the foyer.

"Tonight you have embarrassed us to no end," Booker said.

"I dig. The fuzz had it out for me . . . just because of my unique color. I don't answer to The Man." His fingers traced a box in the air as he said, "Major Squaresville."

"We gave you strict instructions not to smoke in the house," they said together.

"Don't wig out on me. A cat's gotta cool it . . . with his cigs."

"How's this for cool?" said Booker. "We are leaving tomorrow on a family vacation and—"

"Gas! I'd love to cut out for a few days," Airybus interjected.

"You are not going. Period. In fact, we do not want you to step foot in this house while we are gone. Got it?"

At this the brownie made tons of promises (even more outlandish than the ones that got him into the mansion) to make up for the trouble he had caused and to put the Alabaster Mansion and Tarwick Timber Corporation in good financial shape. To the surprise of Booker and Chelsea, the brownie said he had just finished a book that was about to be published. The ugly secretaries had apparently helped in this endeavor. He went on about a book tour and that he would use the profits for the cause of the Tarwicks. This surprised the couple to no end as the brownie didn't strike them as intelligent enough to pen a tome. This promise, like the myriad of others, held little weight.

Booker wrenched the handle on one of the front doors and pointed to the sidewalk. "Out! I don't care about your book or free money. I want you out of this house right this instant!"

"Uh, look . . . that's a real drag, Daddy'O," was the only response as Airybus slunk outside, but not before giving Chelsea a wink as he grooved by her.

VI. Away

A day later the Tarwicks hopped in one of the sport utilities parked in the garage and made their way across leaf-blown freeways and back roads for two hours until they reached their vacation home. They all relished an extended weekend of fishing, watching movies and playing board games in the Northeast. Chelsea was glad to have Booker back and so were the girls.

On the way they realized they had caught the beginning of the fall color change. Booker admitted that he had forgotten how beautiful it was as he peered out the window. Claire said it reminded her of their brownie and his many different colors. She agreed with Jan that they missed him already. He was their little pet.

This disappointed Booker. He was thinking of ways to get rid of the brownie once and for all.

"Hey Claire, just curious, does your Scottish book of strange creatures talk about how to get rid of a brownie once he comes to live in your house?"

"Oh Daddy, you can never kick a brownie out for good. Once he comes to live in a house he is there to stay."

The Tarwicks finally reached their vacation home. Booker punched in the passcode at the gate and the iron gull wings with giant Ts welded in the center, parted in the middle. Once the family had unloaded, Booker checked the electrical and plumbing systems to ensure all was in working order. The worst damage was a few tree limbs that had fallen across the deck skirting the rear of the home.

The first time Booker's cellphone vibrated to life on the marble kitchen countertop, Chelsea snatched it away, powered it down, and hid it in the breadbox. Booker failed to miss the device for another hour and by that time he was laden in plastic jewelry from the Princess Promenade game the girls had him playing. He gave up on calling the office.

They ordered pizza for dinner and then settled into the reclining leather seats of the theatre room to watch TV, huge bowls of popcorn on their hips. And it wasn't just any TV show, of course, but a princess marathon that happened to be on the entire day.

At ten the girls fell asleep in the chairs despite their best efforts to stay up until midnight. Booker and Chelsea each took one in their arms and tucked them into bed without so much as having them change out of their clothes.

Back in the theatre room the parents flicked on a late night talk show. When the commercial was over, they were crestfallen at the image they saw strutting across the hi-def screen. Chelsea spilt the popcorn across the blanket covering her legs. Booker sloshed bottled water over his hand.

There was their little brownie in his cheap suit waltzing over to meet the talk show host. They shook hands and Airybus took a seat to rousing applause from the audience. There was a celebrity persona about him much to the Tarwicks' dismay.

"How'd he do that? How'd he get on a TV show? *How* did he get there?" Chelsea blurted.

"Shhh. Listen. I think he's peddling that book he was talking about. How does he think he can write books?"

Sure enough, on the host's desk was a thin hardback. From its description the book sounded poorly written and boorish. But the crowd lauded it as did the host whom Airybus thanked for the "fall by." The way the brownie paused every four or five words, it seemed like he was reading off a teleprompter. When it obviously malfunctioned, the brownie looked stupid and was unable to annunciate his canned speech.

The audience burst out laughing at the gaff. In effort to recover, Airybus deviated from his script and cracked a few bawdy jokes. He stooped so low as to make fun of retarded people. Next he asserted he was the rightful owner of the Alabaster Mansion and berated the Tarwicks for having ruined the storied home, which he told the world was in extreme debt.

Booker slammed the remote control into the wall. It shattered into pieces. "That little stooge! He says he owns our house? He's yucking it up like he doesn't have a care in the world? He tells the world we're in debt?"

Chelsea, head in hands, was sobbing.

After a sleepless night, Booker and Chelsea got the girls out of bed early. Their protests that they wanted to stay longer fell on deaf ears as Chelsea riffled clothes into their tiny suitcases.

They ate breakfast from a drive-thru on their way back to the Alabaster Mansion. Chelsea drove while Booker frantically checked voicemail and email on his phone. His in-box was full. The CEO could not believe what he was hearing:

COO [Friday, 10:42 A.M.] – "Hey Booker, hate to call when you've just left for vacation, but I just got a jingle from Charles in the hanger. He says a guy came racing up in a 1928 Rolls with two ladies he called his secretaries. The guy told Charles you have given him free reign to take the company's jet. Wanted to go to L.A. Mumbled something about corporate PR. When Charles asked for proof, the guy pulled out your monogrammed briefcase and claimed you gave him permission to discuss corporate matters on the trip. And he had a suit on . . . and he was driving your 1928 Rolls . . . and he flashed the NDA with the new trucking company . . . had you original signature. So Charles called the pilots and let the guy fly. I wasn't informed until the plane was airborne. I'm sorry about all this. Call me to confirm, will ya?"

CFO [Saturday, 7:15 A.M.] – "Listen Booker, just got a call from our institutional bank in New York. There's apparently been some odd activity on all three of our lines of credit. The LOCs have been drawn down to almost nothing. I have no idea what happened and I assume you may know what is behind it. The Treasury Department got the first call. I'm sorry I'm talking so fast. I know this doesn't make sense. Hate to call you so early on a Saturday. You got my cell."

CLO [Saturday, 7:38 A.M.] – "Booker this is Andrew. We have an employment matter we need to discuss. An EEOC claim to be exact. To be really exact, there are a number of claims. I've been getting calls from the heads of HR all morning. It seems—and I don't know how—that someone has been firing the various CEOs of our subsidiaries. Tarwick Mills. Tarwick Cellulose. Tarwick Paper. All of them. He fired them because they were quote—not his color—end quote. He actually said that. We're going to be fighting reverse discrimination claims until we get this cleared up. The guy claims to have been acting under full authority. Wouldn't give a name but the phone lines show he was calling from your house. The man said he was taking over the businesses. This gets even better. The guy who called from your house was speaking like a Beatnik."

Deputy Administrator, FAA [Saturday, 7:44 A.M.]– "Mr. Tarwick, my name is John Hatiey and I am Deputy Administrator of the Federal Administration Association. It has come to our attention that the private jet of Tarwick Timber Corporation has been flying low over the county. Buzzing the tallest buildings, if you will. I have checked with my staff and no one is aware of prior clearance. Given the heightened state of alert for terrorism, this gives us cause for concern. I will be following up with a letter on Monday. I regret to inform you that I will be forced to cite your company under FAA regs. The plane must be grounded until our investigation is complete. Good day."

VII. The Return

Sooner than Booker could respond to those heated voice messages left for him (and numerous others) the sport utility pulled up to the gate of the Alabaster Mansion. The iron gate yawned open and the Tarwicks sped up the long driveway. Chelsea and Booker could not believe their eyes.

A throng of people from all over the county were gathered on the front lawn, shouting in apparent joy and disbelief. At the top of the crowd, near the manse, was their brownie shucking and jiving, throwing handfuls of money to his new best friends.

People were diving, arms outstretched, for all the money being strewn across the lawn. Young and old. Booker recognized the frenzied people as the laziest of the county; those who cared not to work or to get an education. He recognized some as having been let go from the local factories of Tarwick Timber Corp. for an inability to show up at work on time.

Fluttering green bills. Twenties. Fifties. Hundred dollar bills. There was no end to the amount of it. Airybus just flashed his big smile as he tossed it all to the wind.

To Booker's amazement, none of the poor spoke about how they were going to buy food with the money or heat their homes for the winter. The utter disrespect for his money would not have been so heart wrenching if that had been the case. Instead the rabid people bragged how they were going to buy the latest digital gadget and the biggest chrome rims for their tires.

"This is our money," Chelsea was screaming as she dashed to pick it up. Booker was only a few steps away but was unable to hear her over the noise. She then commanded the girls to help out. They thought it was a ton of fun until Jan got her foot stepped on by the thronging mass.

By this time Booker had fought his way through the crowd of revelers. Airybus saw him coming and dashed for the front doors of the Alabaster Mansion.

Booker tore after him.

Inside the brownie skipped up the stairs, two risers at a time, as Booker closed in. The normally staid CEO was yelling obscenities.

On the second floor Airybus made a right and shot into an oval room. Booker followed and began chasing him around in a circle for a number of revolutions with the brownie calling out, "You're such a drag, Daddy'O. Just spreadin' some love and bread to my constituents. A little grease for their palms."

"I'll wring your skinny neck! You hear me? I know it was you and your ugly secretaries who took the corporate jet."

"Smooth ride."

"You buzzed the town!"

"It was really the pilots, not me."

"And you're jealous of our wealth, aren't you? I knew it all along."

"My charisma alone demands that I should be the richest in the county."

"You will leave this house if I have to throw you out by your funny round ears."

A dance move of sorts while going past the door placed the brownie outside the oval room. His dress shoes tapped down the oak stairs and he was back outside in an instant.

Booker fell as he rounded the corner on the second floor and nearly plunged headlong down the stairs. For a moment he caught a glimpse of brown bottles strewn across the foyer below. He recognized them as beer bottles. He saw kidney-shaped stains of dried liquid and enough scuff marks on the normally shiny wood floor to rival any dance studio. It looked like a frat party had taken place in the mansion.

Booker hightailed it down the stairs and raced outside after the creature. He took a handful of steps across the front porch when he heard the front door of the manse slam closed. When he turned around he heard the bolt fall into its moorings with a *thud.*

He spun to find Airybus peering out a sidelight window. At that moment Booker saw what he had failed to notice in all the commotion of flittering money. Black metal grates had been installed across the windows of the Alabaster Mansion. They were bolted into its flashing, yet decorative (*fleur de lys* tips). Regardless, they still gave the manse an appearance of sitting in a bad neighborhood.

As Booker glared through the bars, he saw Airybus holding up a key in one hand. It was a different key than the one on Booker's ring, which he immediately tried to fit in the keyhole. It was now too big. He realized the locks to the front doors had been changed while the family had been away. He raced around the entire structure, trying his key in the multitude of doors to no avail.

The Tarwicks had been locked out of the Alabaster Mansion by their brownie. They could not even smash in a window to gain entrance.

In a beleaguered slump shouldered way he told Chelsea as much upon circling back to the front of the house. The girls were still picking up the last of the money flittering across the front lawn. Booker rounded up the family and led them over to the long garage. Its side door was the only one he had not checked on the grounds.

The key fit and a twist popped the door open. Airybus had missed this one.

Booker flicked on the overheads. He gulped long and hard at what he saw . . . or rather what he didn't see. Only a shiny rubber floor gleamed back at him. The garage had been emptied of his prized antique vehicles.

He raced over to a bank of electronics taking up part of the west-facing wall. He punched buttons and pulled out a keyboard mounted on a slide rack of the built-in desk. Four computer monitors glowed to life before him. They were connected to the many security cameras (some hidden, some plainly visible by design) that were perched in various nooks and crannies of the manse.

Booker reversed the digital video recording to the day they left. Chelsea and the girls huddled behind him in interest. The images on the quartet of monitors moved in unison.

"Stop. Back up. Right there. Look at the monitor for the back portico."

There was a leg, clothed in pinstriped material, climbing in the back window.

"Airybus!" gushed Jan.

Booker slapped a palm to his forehead. "We left the back window open after the fire. That's how he got inside."

Later that day the brownie was captured on video in the foyer drinking cheap beer with two friends he must have invited to the Alabaster Mansion. One of them was also a brownie. And although the video was without audio, Booker could tell that the new brownie was a bombastic loudmouth who acted even stupider than he looked. Nonetheless, his arrogance nearly matched that of Airbus's and as Booker watched in amazement, he reasoned this must be yet another undesirable trait of the creatures.

There they were, the three of them, sliding down the oaken banister, balancing beer bottles on the opposing newel posts, hopping on one leg in a circle, break dancing, holding two bottles on their heads like devil horns.

This embarrassing spectacle infuriated Booker to no end. Since his wild partying days when he whooped it up at an Ivy League university with the kids of other rich families, he had sworn off intoxicants of any kind. This included alcohol and certainly smoking herbs in the greenhouse, of which the brownie had no shame.

The Tarwicks watched in horror as the three drunks snaked around the mansion changing locks and securing metal grates over the windows, zip drills in hand. They were having a great time doing it. High-fives were dolled out and bottles clinked. Little booty-shaking dances were knocked out when they got half the chance.

Then other friends of the brownie showed up with bagfuls of money, which they gave the creature in an apparent exchange for a grand tour of the mansion. There were no levels of depravity to which the brownie would not stoop.

Fast forward another hour and there was the brownie and his saggy secretaries bunkered down in the library, empty bottles lined up across the desk. Airybus had what appeared to be an old fashioned quill in his hand. He signed contract after contract placed in front of him by the secretaries. His name was scrawled in a flamboyant manner with a huge lopsided B and a gigantic O struck through the middle. Even on the video it was apparent he was signing:

Bφφker Tarwick III.

The way he did it reminded Chelsea of the scrawls of a serial killer.

In repetition, he would dip the quill in the inkwell and sign again. He was so happy doing it behind those cabinetknob ears and glowing nose wart.

Booker pointed at the screen. “Those are the letterheads of my companies. He’s signing board resolutions!”

“What?” Chelsea asked. She really could care less about the many companies in the county on which Booker sat on the board of directors.

"Don't you get it? He's taken control of the businesses. He forged my signature!"

"That's funny," exclaimed Claire.

"No it isn't, honey. That's not funny at all. I'm not kidding."

Booker's finger pressed down hard on the keyboard. The images on the quartet of video monitors raced forward. He stopped after two more hours had flickered past. The monitor on the right showed images of the west side of the mansion, near the garage where the family stood.

The brownie was pounding a large sign in the pea gravel driveway.

Clunkers 4 Sale, Cats!

Little Bread!!!

Booker watched in horror as the brownie punched button after button, opening the garage doors. Sitting on each windshield of his prized collection was a white sign. Booker squinted at the screen in search of the missing zeros at the end of the prices. None of the classic vehicles were valued more than the cost of a riding lawnmower.

While Booker sat in shock, Chelsea looked out a garage window.

Outside of the Alabaster Mansion the crush of people remained. They were praising Airybus for giving away all the money of the Alabaster Mansion as he waved from an upper window. To these uneducated lethargic denizens of the county, the brownie offered hope.

VIII. The Fate of the Mansion

Booker raced to the back of the house in a fury. He was not going to get near the crowd. With both fists he thundered on the back door of the mansion.

"Get out here right now, you freakin' brownie! You hear me? Right this instant! This is *my* house."

Booker yanked at the doorknob then the metal grates over the windows. He pounded away; elbows, fists, hips, shoulders all getting a piece of the action. He kicked. Spittle flew from his lips.

For how long he raged at the back of the mansion he would never know for sure. He did it until his toes hurt and shin splints bolted up his legs from kicking the door. He did it until the joints of his fingers and shoulders ached with pain. He did it until lightning bolts shots up his neck. He did it until he could do it no more and slumped onto the slate tiles of the patio feeling useless and used.

After a few moments he noticed Chelsea and the girls crying off to the side in helplessness. None of them had ever seen Booker this way. Not even close in the way he was making—

"Hey!"

Booker thought one of the girls was trying to get his attention. He glanced over at them. They could not even look over at him.

"Hey, what's all the racket?" they heard from somewhere up above. "Cool it, would ya?"

There sat the brownie on the third story balcony in his cheap suit, feet on the railing, round sunglasses on, dragging away on a smoke and blowing O-shaped smoke rings into the crisp fall air. For an instant it struck Chelsea that she and Booker had made love on that very same balcony last fall. And then the fond remembrance vanished—

"I was about to take a nap, dig?"

Chelsea and Claire pointed in astonishment while Jan chanted, "Airybus! Airybus!"

Booker propped himself to his aching knees and then staggered to his feet. He slowly walked from under the portico and squinted up.

"Whoa, you gotta chill, Daddy'O."

Booker tried to refrain his speech. As a result, the order came out with reserve. "Let us back in our house. This little joke has gone too far."

"Your house? Joke? I got news for ya, Daddy'O, this is *my* house now. You don't live here anymore. Out of the goodness of my heart I'll let you come by once in awhile."

Booker heard Chelsea whimpering behind him and that's when he lost it again. "This is OUR house! We invited you to stay with us, remember? Do I need to remind you? It wasn't all that long ago when you pranced up the lawn with that little parade of yours to announce your entrance. You tore up lawn in the process. You sprayed the armpits of my shirts so it looked like I was sweating profusely. You peeked in on Chelsea in the shower and then made her underwear smell like fish."

The brownie tossed his head back and tittered at this.

"You've been smoking who knows what in the house and in front of the girls. In doing so you caught the place on fire and you bounced the basketball at all hours of the night so we couldn't sleep and then got out the golf clubs and . . . and put a hole in the greenhouse window. And we saw you on that talk show—don't ask me how a joker like you got on it—and you were yucking it up like you didn't have a care in the world, making fun of mentally handicapped people while you did it—"

"Man, Booker, don't be so serious."

Chelsea interjected, "You told the world about our financial situation."

That's when the Tarwicks noticed a figure inside the mansion. It was peering from the presidential bedroom on the third floor. They recognized him as the grisly specter of the mansion. A wry grin was stamped across his face and he wagged his tongue at the family. It seemed that even the specter had defected. This pained the family despite Chelsea's ongoing intuition that the ghost was not as loyal to the Tarwicks as he led on all these years.

Booker took to pacing in short bursts—off in one direction and back the opposite way—hands clasped behind him. "And you commandeered the company jet. When you got back you fired my CEOs and changed ownership of my companies. In celebration you invited your buddies over and drank cheap beer throughout the house. You sold my seven figure collection of antique automobiles for pennies on the dollar. You called them clunkers."

"Uh, look . . . the only reason I called them clunkers . . . was because . . . they got low gas mileage. Terrible for the environment, Daddy'O. How are those greenhouse . . . gases, by the way."

Booker heard none of the responses as he paced. "You've locked us out and miserably failed on all of your promises to make the mansion a better place. You've ruined all my hard work. You've caused so much anger and strife."

"Uh, look . . . can't be too much . . . the county gave me a peace prize while you were gone." The brownie fished out of his suit pocket with his left hand (to wit: he was a lefty) a round medal that glinted in the sun as it twisted on its ribbon.

"This is useless. Come on," Booker said to his family.

The Tarwicks left the Alabaster Mansion in disgust that day with full intentions of wresting ownership back into the family by various political and social mechanisms to which Booker Tarwick had access. He would soon learn, however, that he had been forced out of his feted positions within the county, replaced by Airybus to the delight of the poor and the pompous. The Tarwicks would never return to the Alabaster Mansion and lived in relative obscurity in Texas, or perhaps it was Tennessee.

There are those in the county who claim the Alabaster Mansion started to fall into ruin on the day of the Tarwick's departure and still others claim it happened years before under the negligent watch of Booker Tarwick himself. The split is equal among the residents.

What is for sure is that to this very day the brownie can be seen through the barred windows of the mansion strutting up and down the halls, cigarette in hand, laughing and smiling. Occasionally a window will fly open and a fistful of money will be tossed out. The shutters of the mansion are coming unhinged. Shingles have fallen into the rickety gutters that are detaching at the roofline. The columns of the porticos are streaked in filth. The once shimmering alabaster façade has become mottled and stained from lack of care. And if one listens carefully from the street, the brownie can be heard tittering in an evil way from one of the rooms of the decaying Alabaster Mansion.

November 4, 2009

THE BROWNIE OF THE ALABASTER MANSION AFTERWORD

Nineteenth century legends of brownies, those little creatures who take up residence in the quaint cottages of Ireland and the stone houses of chilly Scottish moors, are well documented thanks in large part to the "Ettrick Sheppard" that was James Hogg. It seems these creatures have fallen out of publishing favor (although as real as ever) over the last century and a half, not only in Europe, but most certainly in America if they ever existed at all on these shores.

By this story the feisty brownie has been resurrected through a wonderful literary manifestation called The Short Story. It is my hope that the creature will once again pull up a chair by firesides across the land and take residence in the literature to be forgotten no more. In truth, the brownie has continued to exist apart from the literature over the last century and a half, especially in America. It is only recently, however, that this miserable creature has moved into the Alabaster Mansion.

Afterword²

It is now February 2011 and I have heard from a somewhat reputable woman who is intimately associated with the brownie that he has stopped smoking.

Geblüt Mansion

OPEN LETTER TO MY UNSUSPECTING FRIENDS
FACEBOOK SOCIAL NETWORKING SITE
FEBRUARY 11, 2010
6:48 PM

AS MANY OF you know I grew up in Michigan and I still have a number of family and friends there. A couple months ago I get a call from my ole buddy M_____ who is firmly positioned in the once bright—but now dark and foreboding—real estate business. He tells me the only way to make any money buying real estate in Michigan these days is to snatch one for a song that is in foreclosure. He said he had found the perfect house for pennies on the dollar. To top it off, it was so big it was a sprawling *mansion* more than a house.

"Want to hear the cool part? The place is in Hell!" M_____ told me.

"Good heavens!" I naturally responded. I had heard of this city before, yet had never visited it in my 27 years in the Great Lakes State. I did some research on the Web. The story goes that a farmer named George Reeves was living there with his large family in 1843. He was uneducated and cared little for names of places. When county officials asked Farmer Reeves what he wanted to call the city, he said, 'You can name it Hell for all I care.'"

Now that is a great story. If it isn't true, it should be.

When I asked M_____ why the mansion was being foreclosed, he was unsure. That got my attorney mind racing. I had to research the history of the place. Was it owned by wealthy politicians back in the day? Were fascinating charitable events held on the grounds? Gala banquets in the ballroom? Any grizzly murders? (The macabre side of my personality always asks this about any used house. I've had my suspicions about a few hotel rooms, too.)

Tomorrow, I'll post what my research found: Missing children!

OPEN LETTER TO MY UNSUSPECTING FRIENDS
FACEBOOK SOCIAL NETWORKING SITE
FEBRUARY 12, 2010
7:23 PM

Last month I began my research into the house in Hell, Michigan and zeroed in on a few old newspapers that had been digitized. Turns out the Geblüt family had lived in the mansion since the 1950s when it was built by the great grandmother—Esselté Geblüt—who immigrated to America from some barren region of the Harz Mountains, the highest Northern mountain range in Germany. She was a well-known figure from a highborn family who suddenly left the Harz Mountains to move to this small Michigan city (Hell, no less) for reasons unknown.

I further learned that one of the meanings of the word hell in German is "pale" translated into English. When I saw a photo of Esselté Geblüt in the newspaper, she fit the definition to a T. With her hair pulled back, stark white skin, pointy ears, and full lips there was a vampiric quality about the woman.

Esselté found a husband (Victor) in Michigan and they apparently had four children who all passed away at young ages from a strange "disorder of the neurological system." It was almost like the couple was incompatible; like they were from different *species* that were not meant to intermix. The papers in

Hell were spotty at that time. Yet I learned that Victor died in the seventies, but there was nothing about Esselté. What's more, people had been disappearing in the woods surrounding the mansion for a couple decades. Kids! By connecting all the headlines I found in the digitized papers, the numbers reached into the double digits. Since the disappearances were spread over decades and at different times in the year, investigators had not found a common thread that sewed them together.

The really crazy part is the local rumor that Esselté was a vampire! Geblüt is one spelling of "blood" in German! I wish I hadn't looked that up. When she moved in all kinds of wooden crates arrived from the Harz Mountains with German words stamped on them. A local contractor claimed to have opened one and all there was was dirt inside. Just dirt! The general contractor, a German bloke named Franz H_____, demanded that they use it for the foundation of the mansion. When they were building the mansion the GC made them use every scrap of wood from the crates—doors, chairs. Some were even used for shelves. It all had to be used.

I am known to enjoy a well-done vampire story here and there, but I've never believed any of them. I am a modern man of higher education and reason, after all. My real estate agent/friend M______ (funny how the placement of those titles changed so quickly) said he thought that the executors of the mansion—he had yet to track them down—had been keeping the place up all these years (though doing a poor job of it) and had run out of money. The blood trust fund had gone dry, I guess. He tells me the Geblüt Mansion is going to be auctioned "soon."

"Like how soon is 'soon'?" I asked.

"Saturday. Absolute auction."

"What do you think it will go for?"

"Thirty . . . fifty tops for the 6800 square feet mansion, with five bedrooms, arched stairs, and three fireplaces on forty wooded acres."

"First, you sound way too much like a real estate agent," I told him. "Second, there is no way I can come up with that much cash that quickly."

"Don't worry, Drew. I'll front the cash. If I get it in that price range you'll be the first to know. If you don't want it, one of my other clients will pick it up in a hurry."

"Deal," I said.

OPEN LETTER TO MY UNSUSPECTING FRIENDS
FACEBOOK SOCIAL NETWORKING SITE
FEBRUARY 13, 2010
8:11 PM

To continue with my story, by the following week I got an email from M_____ that he was the high bidder at eighty grand and change. M_____ had it appraised and learned that the mansion and grounds were valued at close to a million. That's right, eighty grand for a place worth nearly a million dollars.

But there was a catch. Isn't there *always* a catch on a good deal? The place needed substantial repairs. M_____, who is more food compactor than building contractor, guessed it to be a quarter of a mill to have a new roof put on, hardwoods laid, energy efficient appliances installed, marble countertops, and to replace the ceilings on the second floor where water damage had occurred. The grounds surrounding the mansion are a mess and many trees (some fallen across the yard and others leaning against the house or with massive limbs that overhung the slate roof) have to be cut up or trimmed back. Even with all that expense I would be up over half a million. Yearly city and county property taxes run north of twenty grand, so I knew I would have to flip it quickly. Maybe I could sell tickets to the haunted vampire house to defray the tax cost in the meantime.

This Thursday, February 15th, I am flying up to Michigan, renting a car, driving 15 miles northwest of Ann Arbor to Hell, and taking a look at the house myself to see how badly it needs repair. If I buy the place I will need to get some contractors in there to fix-it and flip-it (as soon as the Michigan economy turns around). I am not plopping down eighty grand, no matter how good of a deal it might sound, until I have done some heavy due diligence. My real estate agent/friend is vacationing in Barbados so he sent me the key.

This visit is really exciting for me so I've decided to post my first tour of the Geblüt Mansion, this supposed charnel house, live from my cellphone on Thursday.

"LIVE" POSTS TO MY UNSUSPECTING FRIENDS
FACEBOOK SOCIAL NETWORKING SITE
FEBRUARY 18, 2010

9:01 Here goes my live tour from my phone. Gotta love modern technology. Pitch dark. Click on the photos so u can c them.

9:02 (Photo: Snow on Ground) Out of my rental car. Driveway has't been plowed. Going in on foot.

9:03 Walking up the long, winding driveway. I can hear Hell Creek somewhere in the background.

9:03 Flashlite in one hand, typing on phone in the other.

9:05 Freezing out here. I can c my breath.

9:07 (Photo: Trees with Snow) Snow is filling my shoes. Why didn't I bring my boots? I don't miss the North!

9:09 (Photo: Chimney of House) I can c the roofline of rhe mansin above the trees.

9:09 This is so cool.

9:11 Strange quiet in teh woods.

9:11 I only hear the crunch of my shoes, my breething . . .

9:12 Hard typing with one thumb. Pls forgive the spelling.

9:14 (Photo: Front of House) There it is. Take a look at this.

9:15 Icy sidewalk

9:15 (Photo: Doors) Front doors r ancient.

9:16 If my hands will move in this cold I'll try the key M sent me.

9:16 It had better work or Ms paying for my plane tix.

9:17 Yep. Door popped open. Creaky. Rusty hing.

9:17 Whoa. Can't see much but dust.

9:18 (Photo: Chandelier in Foyer) In the foyer. . .

9:20 There's some old furniture covered in tarps. Does that come with?

9:21 (Photo: Stairs) There's an awesome curved stairs. Safe??? I'm heading up.

9:22 Steps moaning. I had beeter not break thru. Not fat. Promise.

9:23 At the top.

9:24 Sneezed from the dust. Not much warmer than outside.

9:25 (Photo: Wrought Iron Balcony) Cool balcony.

9:28 (Photo: Stains on Ceiling) Water stains r all over the ceilings. Major repairs needed.

9:28 House is too quiet. Worse than outside. Creepy. Going to keep moving.

9:29 Stepping over boards, drywall.

9:31 (Photo: Pull-Down Attic Stairs) Stairs to the attic. I'll see the real water damage up there. Why r the stairs pulled down?

9:32 Half way up. Still nothing.

9:32 Awful smell I can't describe. It's getting worse.

9:33 Fetid. Something is rotting up here. More than an animal. Breathing into arm.

9:34 (Photo: Dusty Insulation) Murky up here. Dusty.

9:37 What did I just step on? Sticky. The smell.

9:38 (Photo: Odd Mask) Mask???

9:39 Hard to c.

9:39 (Photo: Dolls on Old Chair) Pile of old dolls?

9:40 (Photo: Bleached Turtle Shell) Skull maybe???

9:41 Someones up here.

9:41 (Photo: Wife in Scarf) Cs me.

9:41 Rfb.

9:42 (Photo: Flashlight Showing Hand with Blood)

OPEN LETTER TO MY UNSUSPECTING FRIENDS
FACEBOOK SOCIAL NETWORKING SITE
FEBRUARY 20, 2010
3:38 PM

There have been many rumors and innuendos surrounding my death by lady vampire in the Geblüt Mansion of Hell, Michigan. I want to put my friends at ease in letting them know that I am back from the dead, or **undead**—so to speak—and doing better than ever.

For those of you who are wondering about all the strange photos and comments on my Wall, I explain: for forty two minutes on February 18, 2010, I clogged up the social networking airwaves with a literary ruse in the grand style of Edgar Allan Poe's "The Facts in the Case of M. Valdemar" or "The Balloon Hoax." For the past week I had been posting how a friend in real estate had gotten a mansion in Hell, Michigan that had been foreclosed. I told how I planned to visit the mansion and would be sending back a feed as I toured the old place, which had links to a lady vampire and people who had disappeared over the years in the 40 acres surrounding the mansion. At the time set I went "live," uploading photos I had stored on my computer every few minutes. The comments were hilarious and I spent those forty two minutes laughing to the point of crying, especially when I uploaded the photo of my wife as the vampire.

Alas egad! Apparently I offended some who thought my untimely death by the teeth of Lady Esselté was real, only to later conclude they may have wasted their time. I am sorry for this. After all, there are many more important things to do on social networking sites like announcing how many pigs you bought at the digital farm and passing out sparkly hearts and shimmering rainbows. Did I mention glittering fish? And let's not forget those photos of animals hugging and florescent pink bunnies in rain-slicks that need to be given away.

Okay, on second thought I am not sorry for having caused this literary brouhaha. I am glad for those of you who were able to experience this with me "live" and I hope you will remember it for some time to come. I have never seen a literary hoax posted before on a social networking site. I plan to publish the entire ruse as it unfolded in my new short collection. It should drop in Q4 of this year. I will keep you—well—posted.

In closing, I sincerely hope *this* post has gone a long way to dispelling those rumors and innuendos surrounding my death by lady vampire. Thanks to all of you who participated (willingly or unwillingly).

GEBLÜT MANSION AFTERWORD

Let's crack open the doors of the Geblüt Mansion, this supposed charnel house of a lady vampire, and take a peek inside at the hoax that was perpetrated within its walls. What is fundamental in pulling off any literary hoax is the gullibility of those who experience the story. After sitting back for a couple months and reading posts on various social networking sites, watching the work of those who post multiple times every day (or *hour*), and the believability by some regarding everything posted by those same people, I realized the door was wide open at the Geblüt Mansion.

In 1844, when America buzzed with talk of a trans-Atlantic balloon flight that was perhaps obtainable given recent long flights in Europe, Edgar Allan Poe had his opening. If successful, a balloon flight would have cut the time it took to cross the Atlantic down to a matter of days as opposed to weeks by ship. Poe took advantage of the public's anticipation and published a story with no title, but which simply began with headlines: "Astounding News! By Express Via Norfolk" in a small daily newspaper called *The New York Sun, Extra.*

The article was not signed and appeared to be from a news reporter. Here's what Poe recounted in "Doings of Gotham - Letter II," *The Columbia Spy* (Columbia, Pennsylvania), May 25, 1844: *On the morning (Saturday) of its announcement, the whole square surrounding the "Sun" building was literally besieged, blocked up — ingress and egress being alike impossible, from a period soon after sunrise until about two o'clock P. M. In Saturday's regular issue, it was stated that the news had been just received, and that an "Extra" was then in preparation, which would be ready at ten. It was not delivered, however, until nearly noon. In the meantime I never witnessed more intense excitement to get possession of a newspaper. As soon as the few first copies made their way into the streets, they were bought up, at almost any price, from the news-boys, who made a profitable speculation beyond doubt.*

What a great story of Poe's eyewitness account to his own literary victims. Oh to have a photo of Poe, from darkened corner watching them come!

Preparation was key for Poe with his balloon hoax. To get started with mine, I typed out the entire script that I would post on the social networking site. For a week prior to my supposed flight to Hell, Michigan to check out the foreclosed mansion that I was going to purchase, I began posting the background of the story that you read above. Or some may call it the introduction to the live event. I spelled out the exact date and time when I would visit the mansion, ensuring that it was during a heavy traffic hour on the social networking site. Weeks before, I hustled around taking photos to upload that would represent my supposed tour of the place. This was done with the enthusiastic assistance of my eight and four-year-old daughters. So, the stage was set . . . yet not entirely. All great hoaxes need an accomplice—a straight man if you will—or in this case straight women. I solicited the services of Cindy Gagne and Julie Todd to comment on my "live" posts in a effort to build the drama. And let's not forget Kyra who reluctantly played the part of Lady Esselté Geblüt.

The photos were dark since my supposed tour of the mansion happened at night. Unfortunately they would not show up well in the print version of this story and they are best left to the imagination.

Next I had to get the timing right on the posts. I calculated how long, for instance, it would take me to walk down the long, winding driveway in the snow before I got a complete glimpse of the mansion.

To make it appear authentic I added spelling errors since I was supposed to be typing on my cellphone's keyboard with my right thumb and carrying a flashlight in my left hand. My phone automatically adds punctuation at the end of sentences. For the ending, when I was attacked by the vampiric monster who is Esselté Geblüt herself, I studied the layout of my phone's keyboard. If my right thumb is on the E or R and the phone slips out of (or is torn from) my hand, my thumb would move diagonally down the keyboard. It would drag across the F or G on the line beneath and then the V or B on the bottom line, as those letters are placed below the F or G, respectively.

Those items in place, I had all the trappings of a literary hoax on my hands and I am just the kind of writer to waste no time in taking full advantage of it!

As I sat at the keyboard in my house, the literary ruse was executed with many excited comments and confusion on the social networking site. I laid low for a few days after the posting and then resurfaced from the dead to let all my friends know I was still alive and kicking.

Most of them were relieved. I am sure a few wished I really had taken it on the neck by the lady vampire from the Harz Mountains.

Stain

June 3, 2006, 6:05 PM
Latitude: -43.666; Longitude: 172.607

THE SIDES OF the pickup rattled as it traveled down the farm roads of Christchurch, New Zealand. It made a staple gun sound as it bottomed. The shock absorbers were shot. A wet June had kept the dust at a minimum yet had revealed an entire population of potholes lurking beneath the top layer of dirt and gravel.

Alexandra "Milky" Wentford was having none of it. "Do you have to hit every one?"

"I'm looking for him, Milky. He's not easy to spot."

The pickup slammed into a rut and bottomed out in a malevolent convenes of metal and road.

"You watch the potholes. I'll watch for the guttersnipe."

Daniel flexed his jaw muscles, but this time said nothing. Whether he talked back, grumbled or made facial gestures, he always responded to Milky's frequent orders, which had only increased in their two decades of marriage. He really didn't care what she said today as long as they found the boy.

Rumors abounded in reference to the homeless kid and how he got to Christchurch. There were those who claimed he ran away from an Australian orphanage and others who said he was the son of an explorer who died on an expedition to Antarctica. It was said the Catholic Church was trying to recruit him into the seminary. Milky had her own theory and Daniel, as was usually the case, held a belief diametrically opposed to that of his wife's.

The pickup, with its rusted wheel wells and fender secured on one side with chicken wire, did not reach over 25 kilometers per hour as Milky scanned wintergreen fields for the boy. He was often seen mulling about a small teashop in the Cathedral Square of Downtown Christchurch. Café New Tealand had taken to feeding him day-old scones.

It had been the first place the Wentfords had looked, to no avail. They checked an Anglican cathedral on the outskirts of town and its adjacent graveyard. They searched in culverts and playgrounds; anyplace that had shelter. They sputtered along the Avon River for three kilometers as Daniel tried to avoid craters in the road and Milky scanned. They even stopped and combed over a construction yard and the giant hollow cylinders of yet to be installed concrete drain pipes. Now they were tracking the country roads leading back to their farmhouse in the rural valley of Hoon Hay.

"Slow down. Slow down!" Milky blurted, pointing. "Over there by the cabbage tree. He's sucking juice from the spines. See him?"

To Daniel the urchin's spiked hair bore a resemblance to the jagged crowns of the tree. "Yeah, that's him." Daniel angled the pickup over to the shoulder and put on the flashers. "You got it?"

"Right in my pocket."

"Think we should both go?"

"You stay put. The looks of you might scare him."

"The looks of *me*?"

Milky gave Daniel a hug. "Another step closer to our dream." She got out and gently closed the door behind her so as not to alarm the boy. She picked her way up a grassy embankment and was nearly at the top when he saw her. The boy turned to run when she called out, "I've got money for you. Lots of it."

He paused and glanced back towards her.

Milky extracted a wad of folded bills from the pocket of her jeans. She flapped them in the air and said her name.

"What's the catch?" the streetwise boy asked.

"My husband and I—he's the one sitting in the pickup—are embarking on a new career of sorts. We need an assistant at our farmhouse."

"For what?"

"A trick of sorts."

The boy crunched his face as he mulled the offer. Finally, "Money up front."

"Half now, half later. Should only take an hour or two. No heavy labor on your part. We'll bring you right back here."

The boy approached Milky and snatched part of the bills. He fanned through them and saw that it was enough to eat well for a month. He stuffed the bills in his pockets.

There was a moment when Milky thought he was going to bolt. Daniel thought the same from his seated position, knowing the chances of him (and his late-forties gut) being able to catch the kid were slim to none.

Yet the boy surprised them. He went over and began making his way down the embankment. He hopped into the bed of the pickup as Milky stood in a bit of shock. This was the first of many things the couple would do that day that they had never tried before.

A hundred potholes later and the pickup swung into the snaking driveway that led to the peeling door of the farmhouse. The door and its appearance was yet another project Milky had been riding Daniel about for months on end. Daniel wanted to get the barn painted first and he had yet to get around to that, either.

The farmhouse itself was constructed by Daniel's father in the nineteen seventies. Its walls were of fieldstone and mullioned windows framed in whitewashed pine. It sat on forty acres of verdant hillocks inset in rocky outcroppings. The Wentfords raised sheep and a few heads of cattle. A couple dairy cows were thrown into the mix. There had been *many* other species at one time or another on the farm thanks to Milky and her ideas of animal raising riches. Minks led to ostriches, ostriches pointed toward emus, emus pushed them to llamas, and llamas to alpacas. The later two leapers (along with constant nagging from Milky) caused Daniel to erect a fence on their acreage that never seemed to be tall enough. Attrition and predators took their toll. They got themselves a year-old Rottweiler to patrol the grounds. Yet, after years of chasing after the latest animal raising craze, the Wentfords found themselves with little to show for it.

It was Milky who decided—after viewing NEW ZEALAND'S ZANY TALENT SHOW on TV—that a career in magic would bring them riches untold. There would be travel. There would be glamour. She could wear sparkling outfits and high-heeled shoes on a nightly basis. Gone would be the muddy hands and boots, hair bound in a handkerchief, overalls and flannels. Milky had it all figured out. They would start playing local venues and then Christchurch proper; perhaps move up to cruise ships and if they were really good, land a spot in Vegas at some venue just off The Strip.

When Daniel swung open the weathering door of the farmhouse, the boy saw a rectangular box made of wood. There were round holes cut into each end. The top of the box was a hinged door swung to the open position. A metallic contraption that appeared to the boy like a giant carrot slicer was mounted on the near end of the box. The entire thing sat on a rustic dinning table that Daniel had made last winter.

"Looks like a coffin," the boy commented.

"Pshaw," Milky blurted. "We think of it as a work of art." She was quick to point out that the long box would be their closing act. The boy was to be their able-bodied assistant. Daniel had designs to hire a nubile young girl for the act. He also had designs to someday tell Milky.

Nevertheless, what startled the boy was not the contraption on the table, but a gruesome head mounted on the near end. It had a lumpy, unearthly face that belonged in a circus sideshow.

"Oh that's Alfie. Made him myself. I'm the cook round here. Alfie's face is nothing more than cheese curds brushed with vanilla to get the light brown color. Alfie likes to be tanned. Alfie's nose is a pork rind, but don't tell him that," giggled Milky. "Alfie's eyes are quail eggs. I found some emu skin out in the barn. Used a strip for the lips. Now the hair . . . my, my the hair," Milky said as she fluffed it. "The hair took me—what would you say, Dan—three weeks? Implanted each individual strand of Emu hair myself. Alfie can't do anything with it in the morning." With that she outright laughed.

The three of them stepped onto the groaning wood-plank floor of the dinning room. Alexandra "Milky" Wentford started to tell the boy of their magical plans and the name they picked out for their dog years ago when they first started thinking of their new career. "Houdini," it was because of the way he hid for days on their property without being seen.

The boy walked over and ran his hands along the box. "You make this?"

"Sure did," Daniel responded in a proud manner. "Built the barn out back, too."

"He's real handy," Milky added. "Now, now you just lie down here in the box, face up, sit on the table if you have to, that's it, that's it, twist those legs over, no, legs at the other end, there, there, ankles into those holes, neck into the one up here, the padding should feel real comfortable, and—"

"You're sure this thing is safe?"

"Very," asserted Daniel as if he was a tad offended by the question.

"Thanks for doing this for us," Milky said to the boy.

Before he knew it her arms were around him in a bear hug. Milky smelled of cheap perfume and hay. When she finally let go, he thought he noticed a joyful tear in her eye.

The boy was thin, but the box hardly fit him as he squirmed into it. He tested the sides. Above him he noticed for the first time the dinning room chandelier made of deer antlers. As Milky began turning down the collar on his shirt to expose his grimy neck, the boy looked up at the glistening blade. "Let me guess, this is one of those head chop tricks. Right? The blade comes down—"

"*Kha-chop!*" exclaimed Milky with a pop to her voice.

Daniel gave off a chuckle. "For all Milky's enthusiasm there is nothing to be worried about, young man." Daniel pointed to a wood stopper. "When the blade falls it hits this piece of wood above your neck and stops. That triggers a hidden blade to drop from the bottom of the box so that it appears the top blade went all the way through. The mannequin head will drop and a black curtain will cover your head. We haven't got the curtain set up yet. I've been too busy on this box-n-blade."

The boy felt uneasy. "You have tested this, right?"

"Tested, tested, oh sure," they both said at once, heads bobbling.

"I can tell you're really into this magic stuff."

"It's going to be our new livelihood," Daniel said.

"Uh-huh, *liveli*hood," came Milky.

The boy stared at the garish mannequin head releasably secured next to him; the pigmented cheese curds, the rancidity of decaying cheese and dried vanilla, the spiraled pork rind nose and its wafting bacon odor, bubbly lips of scored emu leather, eggshell eyes, spiked barnyard animal hair individually placed by Milky into clay.

"Look, Milky, the hair almost matches the kid's. This is good luck."

"Plug straight it is. Now get on with it."

The boy watched the lid of the box fall into place. Craning his neck he saw Milky reach over and snap a rusty pad lock so that he was trapped inside. The box was tight on his chest and it was difficult to suck in a full breath. He next felt his feet begin to tingle at the other end from lack of circulation. Yet it was the sharp pain at the side of his neck that got his full attention.

"Excuse me, but I feel the blade stopper digging into the right side of my neck. My neck's too big for the hole." With that he noticed Daniel give Milky a questioning look.

"It's nothing," Milky informed, "just a little cockeyed." She moved to the head of the box and began pushing on the wood stopper; first one hand, then with both her meaty hands. "It's fine. Fine as pork rind."

"I don't like this," the boy said in a tremulous voice.

"Hush, you little wombat. Right as rain."

"No, something is not right." The boy started wriggling as best he could. His arms were pinned at his sides. The snaking veins above his temples were bulging. "I want out! You haven't tested this!"

"Now, now, you just calm down," Milky ordered. "All according to plan." She pushed harder on the wood stopper and called out, "Do it, Dan. Release the blade."

The long wooden box was vibrating-rocking-sliding on the table; gouges being carved into its surface. The feet end had moved six inches over the edge of the table. Milky stopped her jury-rigging and raced down to slide it back. Unconsciously, out of nervousness more than anything else, Daniel was doing sweeping motions that resembled the traditional Maori dance called the Haka, which he had learned in the military at East Timor.

"Do it, Dan!"

"Let me out! *Now!*"

The blade released.

There was a piercing scream.

Wood splintered.

And two heads fell and landed. Upright. Facing each other. Severed necks sucking to the floor. And in the next pulse of time there flowed from one an unhallowed rush of gore that formed a perfect circle on the wood planks.

June 4, 2006, 1:42 AM

"It's not coming out!"

"Scrub harder. Put some back into it!"

"I am, Milky. I am."

"It will be daylight soon."

Daniel Wentford's hands were beet red from the chemicals and the rough brush handle. Since the rubber gloves had cracked he had gone at the stain using bare hands. He had been scrubbing the plank floor for six hours, on and off; much of the time under the duress of his hovering wife and the thickset bulwark of her shadow.

He tipped over the wooden bucket at his side. Sudsy liquid washed across the planks and his tired shoulders began pumping again. Although the circular stain was only eighteen inches in diameter, an area quadruple the size was soaked in chemicals of every kind imaginable.

Daniel had started with anti-bacterial hand soap. When that substance did little to remove the stain he changed to dishwashing soap. He mixed in the plant extract tutin from the local tutu tree and a nasty sulfur compound from crushed leaves of the stinkwood tree. They had a few on their sprawling property. Daniel next tried the gritty industrial soap used to clean the stalls of the barn—to no avail. Milky insisted on using vinegar. She claimed her old family recipe never failed. Daniel claimed no natural substance would get the stain out. Now the bucket contained a skin-eating mixture of paint thinner, hydrogen peroxide and water.

"On the stain, Daniel. You're missing it."

The thin light of the deer antler chandelier quavered overhead. Daniel paused to a kneeling position and straightened his back. "You want to scrub, Milky? You're more than welcome. There's another brush on the shelf in the barn."

"Oh, Daniel. That kind of talk isn't helping get the blemish out."

"Ncither is your mouth!"

"Harder I tell you!"

As Milky huffed from the room, Daniel went back to work. His lower back throbbed and a pinched nerve was developing in his elbow. His eyes were glazing over from the fumes. The buzz he was getting kept him plying away. The tingling allowed him to tune out Milky.

June 4, 2006, 7:50 AM

Milky stared down at the floor. "I don't understand it. The stain won't come out. How long do you think we can keep it hidden?"

Daniel mumbled something from the corner of the room about the couple's lack of entertainment skills even in their small town and how they would never make it in Vegas. He was sitting on the floor holding his arm in his lap. His hand was a throbbing mass and his fingernails hurt to the cuticles.

"Get up, Dan. Help me move the table back. But first help me drag the area rug out of the family room. It needs to go over the stain then we can set the table on top of it. No one will ever know."

Houdini barked on the outskirts of the farm in a full, satisfied way.

June 4, 2006, 8:22 AM

Milky and Daniel Wentford hovered over the area rug as the morning sun inclined through the mullioned dining room window. In one square of light was the round crimson spot on the rug. The table had been pulled off to the side.

Daniel was the first to speak after countless minutes of staring. "The stain has soaked through."

"It has not. It's all the chemicals you put on it. So much got sucked into the hardwoods that the rug leeched it out. That's all."

"Look at its color, Milky, and it's a perfect circle."

"Maybe the carpet fibers changed the color. That's all. There's a ton of dye in these cheap rugs you buy at the flea market."

Daniel glanced over at his wife. "That's right, it's all *my* fault."

Milky grabbed a corner of the area rug and tried to pull it across the dinning room floor. She quickly realized her husband was standing on it. He was gazing in glassy-eyed amazement at the spot. "Off, Daniel," she snarked. "Instead of standing there like you saw your own ghost, why don't you start ripping up the planks?"

"To rip up these few boards where the stain is wouldn't take me long except my hands and back are killing me."

"I don't want to hear it, Daniel. I'm tired, too. It's not like either of us slept last night."

"The new boards will look . . . new. People will notice."

"You'll have to take up the entire dinning room floor. We'll have cheap carpet laid. That stain is the only evidence left."

By this time Milky was half way across the floor, the area rug dragging behind her.

"Where are you going with that?"

"To burn it with the bones."

June 6, 2006, 2:37 PM

Daniel had the floorboards torn up and stacked for kindling out back. The dinning room had now become a bare cement floor. It was evident that Daniel's father, who built the house with a few of his drinking buddies, was not the most careful of foundation layers. It had been Milky who noticed a slight wave to the surface of the cement, which she never would have noticed in the first place if she was not lying prone to inspect the stain in the middle of the floor.

"Keep scrubbing, Dan. The carpet guys will be here any minute."

The couple had traveled thirty miles to a warehouse DIY store the previous day and ordered the cheapest pad and carpet the place had in stock so they could get next day installation. This was very important in their efforts to hide the stain as quickly as possible.

Daniel, who was on his sixth horsehair brush in three days of scrubbing, had tried every chemical known to modern science (and a few combinations previously unknown) on the ineradicable stain. No matter how much Milky barked at him, he knew the stain would not come out.

Milky leapt to her feet when the knock came at the door.

She opened it to find two burly young men standing there with kneepads strapped around their legs. One had a standard New Zealand accent, which meant Daniel and Milky didn't notice it. The other spoke in the slightly different inflections of an Australian accent.

"Here's the room," Milky announced as the men stepped onto the concrete. "Never mind that spot," she blushed. "Permanent marker leaked through the floorboards. You know how kids never put the caps back on their markers. Those little wombats."

It struck both the men as odd that the stain was being scrubbed by Daniel if it was going to be covered by carpet. One of them produced a digital touchpad and Milky signed the final electronic installation papers as Daniel took a break in the kitchen. Milky gave the installers a big hug.

It took the carpet layers a mere hour to spread and tack the smallish dining room of the farmhouse. Afterward they bagged up the large triangles and parallelograms of leftover carpet and deposited it in the rear of their white van that had WE INSTALL ALL tattooed on the side.

The installer in the passenger seat turned to the driver. "When I was tacking by the kitchen I thought I saw the head of a mannequin . . . on top of the refrigerator . . . just looking at me. Creepiest thing. Spiky hair. A spiral nose. Its face was all bulbous."

"Bulbous? That even a word?" The driver went on to say he had not seen it and besides, the job was finished and they would never have to go back unless there was an installation issue.

They had yet to pull out of the driveway when Milky had the vacuum fired up and was sucking a path through loose carpet fibers sprinkled across the room. A rare smile creased her face as she did it. She was glad to have the stain finally covered up for good and any questions of what happened three nights ago.

Milky was so happy she began carving a giant X over the fresh carpet. *If X marks the spot, then X marks the stain,* she hummed to herself over the whine of the machine. There would be other ways to get out of Hoon Hay and the never ending drudgery of keeping up a farm. She would be famous. She would.

When she got to the center of the X, acrid bile shot up the back of her throat. She raced into the kitchen where she found Daniel applying ointment to his fingers. Milky began pointing at the dinning room in such an agitated fashion that her entire bulwark frame was shaking.

Daniel couldn't understand what she was saying over the noise of the machine. "If a corner of the carpet is coming up I'll tack it down. Just let me rest my hands."

Milky pointed harder.

"Your arm's going to pull out of the socket if you don't stop." Daniel slid back from the kitchen table and peered into the dinning room. "What is it?"

Then he saw the round crimson stain becoming clearer on the new carpet in the fanning light that spread out from the vacuum. Daniel, for the first time in his life, passed out.

Milky was unable to catch him on the way down. A gash was torn into his forehead as it knocked against a corner of the chair rail molding of the dinning room entrance leading into the kitchen.

June 6, 2006, 7:08 PM

It took Daniel longer to pound the FOR SALE BY OWNER sign into the front yard than he would have liked. The pervading darkness and burnt out floodlight secured to the peaked gable of the farmhouse (that he had promised Milky he would change for anon) were not helping matters. Sweat dotted his forehead near the bandage that covered the fresh gash. On the third try he found a patch of ground that did not have rock buried a few inches under the soil. Daniel was right-handed, but that hand was useless from the chemical burns eating at his skin.

June 7, 2006, 7:05 AM

"Put the ottoman over it," Alexandra "Milky" Wentford commanded. "It's just too visible under the dinning room table."

Daniel first got used to taking orders when he served four years (most in Dili, East Timor) with the New Zealand military. He met Milky right out of the service and just kept on taking orders. *From military to Milky*, he often complained to himself. It wasn't all bad. Milky, as her nickname belied, grew up on a dairy farm "pulling and squirting through adolescence," as she described the experience. She had a farmhand's vastness about her with thick limbs to match. It enabled her to help out immediately around Daniel's farm, which he inherited from his parents. They had both died of cancer in the seventies. Two weeks apart. So much for healthy living on the farm.

Part of Daniel was sad to be selling the place—a large part that contained many wonderful childhood memories of fort building and kite flying.

As Daniel got the piece of round furniture from the other room he wondered as to why Milky had picked out carpet lacking crimson tints. She knew about the stain and the extremes they had lodged to keep it covered up. Not a single one of them had worked.

A half an hour later their first potential buyers of the farmhouse, barn, and grounds showed up: Sally and Justin Rankford of Christchurch proper. Milky walked them around the inside of the farmhouse pointing out feature after feature like she had just passed a real estate agent's exam. She had even painted her nails and put on her best pair of jeans and flannel shirt.

When she was through with the "grand tour," Daniel showed the Rankfords out back. Two hundred yards out he referenced the high fence he built to keep the emus from escaping. He pointed out the large earnings potential of the property. The Rankfords wondered whey his hands were bandaged.

Daniel went on to the brook he had diverted a decade ago and pointed out the arched, wooden bridge he had fashioned across its most narrow point. There were the two ruinous tractors his father had owned. One of them had been painted pink in one of Milky's schemes to make farming "more female friendly." She had sketched out an entire line of farming equipment for the female farmer that her and Daniel never got off the ground for lack of funding. The Rankfords noticed the once pink tractor was now the color of aging blood. Daniel promised to remove it as part of the deal.

The barn was last. Daniel could tell Justin Rankford was excited about having a tool room for woodworking projects he had on tap. While Justin went on and on about his lathe. Houdini the Rottweiler jumped out of the hay with a gnawed, longish bone in his mouth that struck Justin Rankford as being almost human in appearance.

Naw.

When they got inside Milky had a purchase agreement laid out on the dining room table that she had downloaded off the Internet. The Wentfords quickly realized that the placing of the agreement on the dining room table as a big mistake. The paperwork brought attention to the table *and* the ottoman beneath it, which Sally Rankford thought was unique placement for a piece of furniture. Milky tried to pass it off as a footrest.

And if Sally Rankford had not noticed the ottoman under the dinning room table, she would not have commented on the stain that sent Milky caterwauling in anguish from the farmhouse while Daniel was left standing there trying to explain the blotch spreading in a circular fashion on top of the ottoman.

February 8, 2009, 12:30 PM

The Christchurch bankers, clad in dark blue suits as if there were any other color for their profession, stood in front of the rustic farmhouse. Bruce Thomlinson was tracing his finger along the foreclosure sign while Joseph Paddington thumbed a stack of papers secured to his clipboard.

To say that the bank's auction of the foreclosed property it now owned had gone poorly was a huge understatement.

"Not *one* person so much as offered up a bid?" questioned Joseph, the senior loan officer.

"It's useless for a house. The place would have to be demolished. The barn could be converted to a mother-in-law's suite, if Granny doesn't mind the constant smell of the animals that had lived there."

Joseph stopped leafing through the financial papers long enough to point at one of the front windows that seemed to be smiling at them with jagged teeth the way it was shattered. The streaks of black char streaking the sides of the translucent mouth gave it the messy appearance of a kid who had just downed a chocolate chip cookie. "What happened there?"

"All sorts of rumors around Hoon Hay. The most popular is that the guy who owned the place blew himself up in a chemical explosion. It torched the dinning room but left the foundation intact."

"Why was he using chemicals in the dining room of all places?"

Bruce retorted, "Oh, it gets better. The wife is said to have gone insane, too. Rolled down the side of Mount Hutt with her arms wrapped around a piece of furniture. An ottoman I think the paper said. The rocks smashed her and the ottoman to a pulp, then—"

Bruce stopped himself to answer the call of his cellphone, which he fished out of his suit coat pocket. "Thomlinson . . . Oh, yeah, it's very available. There were no takers for the absolute auction. . . not anywhere near a subdivision . . . off by itself . . . forty acres . . . uh, huh . . . some trees . . . not bad . . . listen, if you've found a horse track development group that has checked out *and* they've made that kind of offer, take it now . . . sure."

Bruce tucked away his phone and grinned at Joseph.

August 18, 2009, 9:51 AM

The demolition crew had gotten the barn torn down without a hitch. The rusted tractors with their flat knobby tires had been drug off the property. There had been talk of imploding the farmhouse, but a local Hoon Hay ordinance prevented the use of explosives in the rural city to prevent the startling farm animals "who might break down fences and ruin gardens." So the demolition team bulldozed the farmhouse after ensuring that the electricity lines, water taps, and gas feeds had been disabled.

The speediness of the demolition by the crew hired by Equine Racing Group resulted in the construction of the horse racing track to begin on schedule. It ended that way, too. The first race on the track was full of pomp and circumstance with Hoon Hay dignitaries of every sort in attendance. There was even a Hollywood actress from New Zealand in the crowd, wide-brimmed hat rivaling anything seen above a tall mint julep and below the grandstands of the storied Kentucky Derby.

A bugle call, which sounded rather close to "My Old Kentucky Home" to those who had actually been to the Derby, started the ceremonies. A couple of officials spoke as did the president of Equine Racing Group. The horses were led into their stalls. There was a palpable excitement in the air.

The gun sounded and a wisp of smoke spiraled into the air.

The gates thudded open.

BloodThief bolted out of the shoot. At 3-to-1 odds he was one of the favorites. His jockey settled into his crouch and applied the riding crop. At the quarter mark BloodThief had built a full length advantage.

On the inside track, however, charged a black stallion named Twilight Joke. It was gaining fast on BloodThief as the horses rounded the final quarter of the track, hooves churning up the rich Hoon Hay soil, teeth bared, nostrils flaring.

The catastrophe happened so quickly that no one in the stands, even those with binoculars pressed to their eye sockets, could tell that it was Twilight Joke who lost his footing. He did it at such an angle in rounding the corner that his sleek muscular torso carried him from the inside track toward the middle of the track. This was right into traffic.

Twilight Joke felled two other stallions in a throbbing mass of splayed legs, toppling jockeys and spindling hooves. Human and equine bodies lay strewn across the track. Emergency workers mobilized and drove to them in a whir of flashing lights. They surveyed the injuries: three horses, five broken legs. The jockeys lay moaning in pain.

Minutes later the crowd gasped in horror, backs turned, as they heard a gun blast issue three more times.

May 1, 2025, 11:42 AM

Legend and lore surrounding the failed horse racetrack in Hoon Hay, New Zealand stretched nearly as long as the number of months since it was last used for any type of commercial endeavor. That was back in 2009. The track closed after the first race was held on its soil, never to be used again; now a litter-blown, graffitied blight on the pastoral landscape.

The first developer of the property in over fifteen years was cognizant of the legends and lore surrounding the failed racetrack. When a kid, Curt Livingstone had sung a poplar and horrific rhyme while playing on his favorite Christchurch playgrounds. Being an adult with construction project responsibilities and the headaches that invariably go along with them, he paid the hauntings of his youth little mind as he surveyed the diagram for the skyscraper project. He could not help thinking how much the once rural city of Hoon Hay had changed.

Before him the massive concrete foundation for the skyscraper was about to be poured into a gridwork of rebar and hollow steel walls secured eighty feet into the ground. A convoy of rotund cement trucks was backed up to the crater with metal troughs extended;

each driver awaiting the signal from Livingston's supervisor to start pouring.

Looking up from his architectural diagram one last time, Livingston saw his Columbian supervisor running toward him. He was pointing toward the rectangular crater.

"The stain is there! Right in the middle of moorings." The Columbian crossed himself. "No matter how deep we dig it's there. It's a bad omen, Boss. We should not pour over the stain. The legend is right."

This gave Livingston pause. The fears of his childhood came rushing back to him in fits.

THE STAIN WON'T GO AWAY.

Didn't it repeat twice . . . at the end?

THE STAIN WON'T GO AWAY.

THE STAIN WON'T GO AWAY.

Livingston tried to remember the rest of the children's rhyme that is well-known in Hoon Hay to this day. *Something about deep in the earth . . . the farmers. Down to hell.* Once the first line popped into his mind the rest came easily:

IN THE EARTH AN EVIL GROWS,
DEEP IN THE DIRT IT SINKS YOU KNOW,
DOWN TO HELL WHERE IT BELONGS
KILLED THE HORSES FELLED HEADLONG.
THE STAIN WON'T GO AWAY.
THE STAIN WON'T GO AWAY.

THERE WAS A FARMHOUSE OVER THE SPOT,
WHERE FARMERS CAST THEIR MAGICAL LOT,
TO DO THE TRICK THEY WERE FAIN,
UNTIL IT DROVE THEM BOTH INSANE.
THE STAIN WON'T GO AWAY.
THE STAIN WON'T GO AWAY.

"Boss? What should we do? The trucks are all here. The crew is waiting. You tell me 'the day is only as long as the dollars we have to spend.' The stain, sure enough."

Livingston issued the order through gritted teeth, "Pour anyway!"

HOON HAY DAILY

The Noon Day News of Hoon Hay

August 19, 2009

EQUINE RACING TRACK – Congratulations and cheers were the top of yesterday at the ribbon cutting ceremony of Hoon Hay's first horse racetrack. Many dignitaries were on hand for the start of the race. The race, however, quickly played a dour note when three horses suffered broken legs in a terrible crash rounding the final bend. All three horses had to be put out of their misery on the track. Animal rights activists plan a rally today at noon. One jockey was paralyzed and two others remain in the hospital. In surveying the cause of the accident, a viscous stain was found on racetrack. The stain is being analyzed, but is apparently very difficult to remove as it is more than a surface anomaly. A core sample of the ground has been taken. We will continue to follow this tragic story.

June 4, 2091, 09:23 AM
Latitude: 43.666; Longitude: -7.393

Jolando and Rondaré, barefooted and bronzed, kicked the soccer ball down Raizor Beach as they worked up a give-n-go play they were preparing to unfurl on an unsuspecting opponent in next

Saturday's game. Off to the side a citrus sun was rising in full splendor, reflecting off the glazed window balconies they called *galerías* in Coruña, Spain.

The Atlantic Ocean was particularly calm this day. Jolando and Rondaré had plans to strip off their T-shirts and go for a dip as they usually did after practicing in the powdery sands of Raizor Beach. The Tower of Hercules loomed in the distance. The scaffoldings and cranes surrounding the world's oldest surviving lighthouse indicated its first substantial refurbishment in 400 years.

While the ball zigzagged between them, Jolando told Rondaré in a quick Spanish flurry that he had read about a place called Hoon Hay, New Zealand that was an antipode of Coruña, Spain.

"What's an antipode?" Rondaré questioned. He was not the studious one.

"If you drill a hole straight through the earth you will hit that city in New Zealand. That's an antipode."

"So they're upside down and we're right side up."

"Or the other way around," Jolando commented.

Rondaré cared less. He stopped the ball with the bottom of his foot and flicked it up in the air. A chest-trap below his white coral necklace preceded a thigh juggling act. A header sent the checkered ball past Jolando who raced to retrieve it.

When he got over the ball Jolando froze out of curiosity. It quickly turned to revulsion. He saw in the sand a perfectly round bloodspot, the dark color of claret, percolating up to the surface.

STAIN
AFTERWORD

This is perhaps the most horrific tale in the collection, where the verticality of evil is explored in a new way in the literature.

Daily we are bombarded by detergent companies claiming their products can lift any stain. We are no stranger to movies where the murderer tries to hide a blood stain to avoid detection. But what if the evil does not stop on the surface? What if it is more than just a superficial residue of molecules that can be attacked by stain-fighting chemicals?

I believe that true evil cannot be simply wiped away in an infomercial by a guy with a grating voice. Evil has a continuum in the intangible spiritual world and in the tangible physical world. In this story it has a physical verticality.

The seeds of this notion germinated when, in my late teens, I was told by my father (in no uncertain terms as the black viscous liquid drained from the rust bucket that was my 1973 Mustang fixer-upper) that I should never dump used oil on the ground. There were proper ways to dispose of it. In my brash way of responding, which at that time usually consisted of one word statements and questions, I profoundly asked, "Why?" To which I was told that oil does not stay on the surface, but sinks deep into the ground where it can infiltrate fissures of water. This axiom of viscous liquids stayed with me.

In 2009 I began writing this story about an evil stain that does not remain on the surface, but continues sinking until it hits the other side of the planet. For dramatic effect I had to place the stain on a part of the earth so that it would hit land on the other side. There were fleeting thoughts of having it surface under a ship in the middle of the Pacific, but that would neither have the same effect nor be as believable. The stain could not channel through miles of ocean without being diverted in its currents.

Enter the antipode. What if the stain happened at one of the few places on earth that connects to land on the other side of the globe so that if this antipode path were followed, people wholly unconnected to the story would come in contact with the perpetuating stain. Because the earth is mostly water, there are only a few places where if you stuck a pole through the globe at one point it would hit terra firma on an opposite point. That is why Hay Hoon, New Zealand (latitude: -43.666; longitude: 172.607) was chosen as the place where the stain begins and Coruña, Spain (latitude: 43.666; longitude: -7.393) as the antipodal where it ends.

Other Titles by Andrew Barger

Coffee with Poe
A Novel of Edgar Allan Poe's Life

Coffee with Poe brings Edgar Allan Poe to life within its pages as never before. The book is filled with actual letters from his many romances and literary contemporaries. Orphaned at the age of two, Poe is raised by John Allan—his abusive foster father—who refuses to adopt him until he becomes straight-laced and businesslike. Poe, however, fancies poetry and young women. The contentious relationship culminates in a violent altercation, which causes Poe to leave his wealthy foster father's home to make it as a writer. Poe tries desperately to get established as a writer but is ridiculed by the "Literati of New York." The Raven subsequently gains Poe renown in America yet he slips deeper into poverty, only making $15 off the poem's entire publication history. Desperate for a motherly figure in his life, Poe marries his first cousin who is only thirteen. Poe lives his last years in abject poverty while suffering through the deaths of his foster mother, grandmother, and young wife. In a cemetery he becomes engaged to Helen Whitman, a dark poet who is addicted to ether, wears a small coffin about her neck, and conducts séances in her home. The engagement is soon broken off because of Poe's drinking. In his final months his health is in a downward spiral. Poe disappears on a trip and is later found delirious and wearing another person's clothes. He dies a few days later, whispering his final words: "God help my poor soul."

To give us a historical fiction look at Edgar Allan Poe is great. The start where we are at his mom's funeral gives a little insight into why he may write the way he does. It is very interesting the ideas the author has put into the story about Poe. I like the idea of detailing the life of Edgar Allan Poe into a historical fiction novel." . . . "A great idea to give us some insight into why Poe may be the way he is.

AMAZON BREAKTHROUGH NOVEL AWARD EXPERT REVIEWER

The Best Horror Short Stories 1800-1849
A Classic Horror Anthology

The Best Horror Short Stories 1800-1849 is a book for anyone who loves a classic horror story. Thanks to Edgar Allan Poe, Honoré de Balzac, Nathaniel Hawthorne and others, the first half of the nineteenth century is the cradle of all modern horror short stories. Andrew Barger, the editor, read over 300 horror short stories and compiled the dozen best. A few have never been republished since they were first published in leading periodicals of the day such as *Blackwood's* and *Atkinson's Casket*. At the back of the book Andrew includes a list of all short stories he considered along with their dates of publication and the author, when available. He even includes background for each of the stories, author photos and annotations for difficult terminology.

'The Best Horror Short Stories 1800-1849' will likely become a best seller . . .What makes this collection (of truly terrifying tales!) so satisfying is the presence of a brief introduction before each story, sharing some comments about the writer and elements of the tale. Barger has once again whetted our appetites for fright, spent countless hours making these twelve stories accessible and available, and has provided in one book the best of the best of horror short stories. It is a winner.
AMAZON TOP TEN REVIEWER

Through his introduction and footnotes, Barger aims for readers both scholarly and casual, ensuring that the authors get their due while making the work accessible overall to the mainstream.
BOOKGASM

[a] top to bottom pick for anyone who appreciates where the best of horror came from.
MIDWEST BOOK REVIEW

The Best Ghost Stories 1800-1849
A Classic Ghost Anthology

Ghost stories became very popular in the first half of the nineteenth century and this collection by Andrew Barger contains the very scariest of them all. Some thought too horrific were published anonymously like “A Night in a Haunted House” and “The Deaf and Dumb Girl,” with the later being anthologized for the first time since its original publication in 1839. The others included in the fine collection are by famous authors. “A Chapter in the History of a Tyrone Family,” by Joseph Sheridan le Fanu; “The Spectral Ship,” by Wilhelm Hauff ; “The Mask of the Red Death” by Edgar Allan Poe, “The Old Maid in the Winding Sheet,” by Nathaniel Hawthorne; “The Tale of the German Student,” by Washington Irving; “The Legend of Sleep Hollow,” by Washington Irving; and “The Tapestried Chamber,” by Sir Walter Scott. Andrew Barger has added his familiar scholarly touch to this collection by including annotations, story backgrounds, author photos and a foreword titled “All Ghosts Are Gray.”

Edgar Allan Poe
Annotated and Illustrated
Entire Stories and Poems

For the first time in one compilation are background information for Poe’s stories and poems, annotations, foreign word translations, illustrations, photographs of individuals Poe wrote about, and poetry to Poe from his many romantic interests. Here is a sampling of the tales and poems included: “Annabel Lee,” “The Bells,” “The Black Cat,” “[The Bloodhounds],” “The Cask of Amontillado,” “The Conqueror Worm,” “A Descent into the Maelstrom,” “The Fall of the House of Usher,” “The Gold-Bug,” “The Haunted Palace,” “Lenore,” “The Masque of the Red Death,” “MS. Found in a Bottle,” “Murders in the Rue Morgue,” “The Oblong Box,” “The Pit and the Pendulum,” “The Premature Burial,” “The Purloined Letter,” “[The Rats of Park Theatre],” “The Raven,” “Some Words with a Mummy,” “The Swiss Bell-Ringers,” “The System of Doctor Tarr and Professor Fether,” “The Tell-Tale Heart,” and “Thou Art the Man.” The classic illustrations are by Gustave Dore and Harry Clarke, with a great introduction by Andrew Barger.

Andrew Barger opens his hefty book that includes all of the prose and poetry of Edgar Allan Poe with an introduction 'Demystifying Poe', an essay so well written and informative that it sets the tenor for the important collections of his book EDGAR ALLAN POE ANNOTATED & ILLUSTRATED ENTIRE STORIES & POEMS: 'Edgar Allan Poe is arguably our most important original and brilliant author of American letters and most misunderstood. His combination of industriousness, minuteness for detail, originality, and respect for his craft are unparalleled.' Barger then proceeds to offer all of the written works of Poe (many of these will be discoveries to the casual Poe reader), offering annotations to clarify the time and setting and influences on each work. This is an ambitious work and one that immediately becomes the scholar's gold standard for research on this major writer of mystery and thrills.

If for no other reason than to have a solid selection of the works of Poe on the shelf, this beautifully designed and handsomely printed book will serve that intent. But once the reader thumbs through this book, pausing to re-read favorites such as 'The Fall of the House of Usher', 'The Murders in the Rue Morgue', 'The Pit and the Pendulum', and 'The Raven', there are many little known gems of short stories, articles, essays, and poems in addition to the stories that are less familiar to the larger audience to discover.

Barger adds 'guidance' to his method of presenting these works by such devices as listing all of the poems under the subheadings of 'Women in Edgar Allan

Poe's Life', 'Miscellaneous Poetry both Before and After Age 25', 'Autobiographical', and 'Men in Edgar Allen Poe's Life.' These may seem like minor adjustments to the collections, but in Barger's hands the divisions add meaning and context to the works.

In addition to all of the written works of Poe, this handsome book contains photographs and many of the famous illustrations for his works - especially those of Harry Clarke and Gustave Dore. The fine art of these two men is also honored with annotations adding to their importance to Poe's popularity as a writer. This is simply a splendid book, handsomely written and produced, and a fine tribute to the literature of Poe - and to the scholarship of Andrew Barger! Highly Recommended.
AMAZON TOP TEN REVIEWER

Leo Tolstoy's 20 Greatest Short Stories Annotated

"Anna Karenina" and "War and Peace" revealed Leo Tolstoy as one of the greatest writers in modern history. Few, however, have read his wonderful short stories. Now, in one collection, are the greatest short stories of Tolstoy, which give a snapshot of Russia and its people in the late 19th century. Annotations are included of difficult Russian terms. Read these short classics today!

Now for the first time, twenty of his best short stories have been compiled and edited into a single volume by Andrew Barger. Enhanced for the reader with informative annotations. The stories comprising this outstanding collection include: A Candle, After the Dance, Albert, Alyosha the Pot, An Old Acquaintance, Does a Man Need Much Land?, If You Neglect the

Fire You Don't Put It Out, Khodinka: An Incident of the Coronation of Nicholas II, Lucerne, Memoirs of a Lunatic, My Dream, Recollections of a Scorer, The Empty Drum, The Long Exile, The Posthumous Papers of the Hermit Fedor Kusmich, The Young Tsar, There Are No Guilty People, Three Deaths, Two Old Men, and What Men Live By. A truly impressive anthology, "Leo Tolstoy's 20 Greatest Short Stories" is especially recommended for acquisition by community and academic libraries, as well as the supplemental reading lists for students of Russian Literature.
MIDWEST BOOK REVIEW

The Best Werewolf Short Stories 1800-1849
A Classic Werewolf Anthology

Andrew Barger has compiled the best werewolf stories from the period when werewolf short stories were first invented. The stories are "Hugues the Wer-Wolf: A Kentish Legend of the Middle Ages," "The Man-Wolf," "A Story of a Weir-Wolf," "The Wehr-Wolf: A Legend of the Limousin," and "The White Wolf of the Hartz Mountains." It is believed that two of these stories have never been republished in over one hundred and fifty years since their original printing. Read "The Best Werewolf Short Stories 1800-1849" tonight, just make sure it is not by the light of a full moon!"

Knowledgeably compiled and deftly edited by Andrew Barger, "The Best Werewolf Short Stories 1800-1849: A Classic Werewolf Anthology" is a 170-page literary compendium covering a fifty year span from 1800 to 1849 and identifying famous and not-so-well known authors who wrote werewolf stories . . .. After an informed and informative introduction on

the subject by Andrew Barger, five of these stories are presented in full, followed by a listing of short stories considered from 1800 to 1849, along with an index of Real Names. A seminal work of impressive scholarship, "The Best Werewolf Short Stories 1800-1849: A Classic Werewolf Anthology" is highly recommended reading for fantasy fans, and a valued addition to academic library Literary Studies reference collections.
MIDWEST BOOK REVIEW

Connect with Andrew Online:

Website: AndrewBarger.com

Blog: AndrewBarger.blogspot.com

Amazon: Andrew Barger on Amazon

Friend him on Facebook:
www.facebook.com/Andrew-Bargers-Official-Facebook-Page

Fan him on Goodreads:
http://www.goodreads.com/author/show/1362598.Andrew_Barger

Follow him on Twitter:
http://twitter.com/andrewbarger

Bottletree®

BottletreeBooks.com

www.ingramcontent.com/pod-product-compliance
Lightning Source LLC
Chambersburg PA
CBHW030426310726
48979CB00009B/1644/J

* 9 7 8 1 9 3 3 7 4 7 2 7 9 *